Nestled on the rugged town of Penhally. Wi landscapes and a warm lucky tourist who stumb

But now Mills & Boon® Medical™ Romance is giving readers the unique opportunity to visit this fictional coastal town through our brand-new twelve-book continuity… You are welcomed to a town where the fishing boats bob up and down in the bay, surfers wait expectantly for the waves, friendly faces line the cobbled streets and romance flutters on the Cornish sea breeze…

We introduce you to Penhally Bay Surgery, where you can meet the team led by caring and commanding Dr Nick Tremayne. Each book will bring you an emotional, tempting romance—from Mediterranean heroes to a sheikh with a guarded heart. There's royal scandal that leads to marriage for a baby's sake, and handsome playboys are tamed by their blushing brides! Top-notch city surgeons win adoring smiles from the community, and little miracle babies will warm your hearts. But that's not all…

With Penhally Bay you get double the reading pleasure… as each book also follows the life of damaged hero Dr Nick Tremayne. His story will pierce your heart—a tale of lost love and the torment of forbidden romance. Dr Nick's unquestionable, unrelenting skill would leave any patient happy in the knowledge that she's in safe hands, and is a testament to the ability and dedication of all the staff at Penhally Bay Surgery. Come in and meet them for yourself…

Dear Reader

When I was approached to by my editor to write Book Seven of the **Penhally Bay** continuity I was really thrilled, as I love writing about small communities where everyone knows everyone. But in this case my heroine, Eloise Hayden, is a total newcomer to the tiny village, and has the very difficult task of finding out the truth behind a fellow Australian's death. There are very few of us who enjoy being pushed out of our comfort zone, and poor Eloise soon finds herself struggling to maintain her professional armour when she meets the handsome and newly single Chief Inspector Lachlan D'Ancy! No matter how hard she tries to be all stiff and formal he only has to smile at her and she totally melts. Don't you just love heroes like that?

I really enjoyed writing this novel as it offered me a challenge to intricately research the role of a forensic pathologist. The dedicated and painstaking work they do is integral to solving crimes and suspicious deaths, thereby giving much needed answers to loved ones. Like Eloise, I was certainly out of my comfort zone a few times during the writing of this story, but as I typed 'The End' I had a smile on my face—and I hope you do too.

Happy reading

Melanie Milburne

SINGLE DAD
SEEKS A WIFE

BY

MELANIE MILBURNE

⊚ ™ MILLS & BOON ®
Pure reading pleasure

A very special thank you to Dr Robert Kelsall MBBS (Adelaide)
FRCPA MBBS(Perth) Ad Eundem Gradum, whose extensive forensic
experience was invaluable in the researching of this novel. Rob, I literally
could not have done it without you. Also to Sergeant Iain Roy Shepherd
who, like Rob, is always just a phone call or e-mail away.
My heartfelt thanks to you both.

First published in Great Britain 2008
Harlequin Mills & Boon Limited,
Eton House, 18-24 Paradise Road, Richmond, Surrey TW9 1SR

© Melanie Milburne 2008

ISBN: 978 0 263 86326 0

Set in Times Roman 10½ on 12¾ pt
03-0608-50312

Printed and bound in Spain
by Litografia Rosés, S.A., Barcelona

Melanie Milburne says: 'I am married to a surgeon, Steve, and have two gorgeous sons, Paul and Phil. I live in Hobart, Tasmania, where I enjoy an active life as a long-distance runner and a nationally ranked top ten Master's swimmer. I also have a Master's Degree in Education, but my children totally turned me off the idea of teaching! When not running or swimming I write, and when I'm not doing all of the above I'm reading. And if someone could invent a way for me to read during a four-kilometre swim I'd be even happier!'

Recent titles by the same author:

Medical™ Romance
THE SURGEON BOSS'S BRIDE
HER MAN OF HONOUR
IN HER BOSS'S SPECIAL CARE
A DOCTOR BEYOND COMPARE
  (Top-Notch Docs)

Did you know that Melanie also writes for Modern™ Romance? Her stories have her trademark drama and passion, with the added promise of sexy Mediterranean heroes and all the glamour of Modern™ Romance!

Modern™ Romance
WILLINGLY BEDDED, FORCIBLY WEDDED
BOUGHT FOR HER BABY
BEDDED AND WEDDED FOR REVENGE
THE VIRGIN'S PRICE

BRIDES OF PENHALLY BAY

Bachelor doctors become husbands and fathers—
in a place where hearts are made whole.

At Christmas pregnant Lucy Tremayne
was reunited with the man she loved
Christmas Eve Baby by Caroline Anderson

We snuggled up in January
with gorgeous Italian, Marco Avanti
The Italian's New-Year Marriage Wish by Sarah Morgan

Romance blossomed for Adam and Maggie in February
The Doctor's Bride by Sunrise by Josie Metcalfe

Single dad Jack Tremayne
found his perfect bride in March
The Surgeon's Fatherhood Surprise by Jennifer Taylor

In April a princess arrived in Penhally!
The Doctor's Royal Love-Child by Kate Hardy

In May Edward Tremayne found the woman of his dreams
Nurse Bride, Bayside Wedding by Gill Sanderson

Attend gorgeous Chief Inspector Lachlan D'Ancey's
wedding this June
Single Dad Seeks a Wife by Melanie Milburne

The temperature really hots up next month—
Dr Oliver Fawkner arrives in the Bay…
Virgin Midwife, Playboy Doctor by Margaret McDonagh

In August Francesca and Mike
try one last time for the baby they've longed for…
Their Miracle Baby by Caroline Anderson

September brings sexy Sheikh Zayed
to the beaches of Penhally
Sheikh Surgeon Claims His Bride by Josie Metcalfe

Snuggle up with dishy Dr Tom Cornish in October
A Baby for Eve by Maggie Kingsley

And don't miss French doctor Gabriel,
who sweeps into the Bay this November
Dr Devereux's Proposal by Margaret McDonagh

A collection to treasure for ever!

CHAPTER ONE

'I'M VERY sorry, Dr Hayden, but your luggage seems to have gone missing without trace,' the baggage official informed Eloise as he looked up from the computer in front of him. 'There's no record of it even being loaded on your flight.'

'*Missing?*' Eloise glared at the young man. 'What do you mean, it's missing? I was supposed to be in Cornwall twenty-four hours ago. I can't hang about here waiting for my things to arrive on another flight from Sydney. You'll have to send them on to me.'

'That won't be a problem, Dr Hayden,' the young man answered, reaching for a pen and the necessary documentation. 'The airline will pay for delivery under these circumstances. Do you have the address of where you will be staying?'

Eloise suppressed a frustrated sigh and rummaged in her handbag for the name and address of the guest-house she had been booked into in Penhally Bay. As far as rating stars went, Trevallyn House looked like it was missing a few, but, then, that was the Australian Health Department budget for you, she thought cynically. Her superiors had told her a month in a Cornish seaside town should more than compensate for any discomfort from staying in a building that looked as if Captain Cook himself had dropped in on his way to Botany Bay in 1770.

She gave the man the brochure with the address on it, and also her own card, and tapped her foot impatiently as he took the relevant details. 'How soon do you think it will be located?' she asked as she took back the guest-house brochure.

The man gave a little shrug. 'It could be a day or two, maybe longer. It's hard to tell. It must have been put on the wrong flight in Sydney. It happens occasionally.'

Eloise mentally rolled her eyes. 'Well, it's nice to know my luggage gets to do a round-the-world tour, but I really would like you to do what you can to locate it and quickly. I've been in these clothes for close to thirty-six hours. I'm on official business so I need to have access to my luggage as soon as possible.'

'I'll do everything I can to speed things up but, as I said, it might take time,' he said. 'The increased security at airports has eased some problems but created others, as I am sure you will understand.'

Eloise gave him a small tight smile. 'Thank you for your help,' she said. 'I will look forward to hearing from you.'

She made her way out of the busy terminal to the hire-car pick-up area where after another long wait she was finally assigned to one of the tiniest cars she had ever seen.

'I'm going to kill you with my bare hands, so help me, God, Jack Innes and Co,' she said under her breath as she drove out of the parking lot. 'Just as well my luggage didn't arrive. Who knows where I would have put it.'

Penhally Bay was a typical Cornish village. There were picturesque houses and shops lining the streets overlooking the harbour and there were loads of tourists milling about, taking advantage of the warm summer weather. There was a lifeboat station at one end of the bay and a lighthouse at the other and as Eloise looked out to sea she could see several boats and their crews enjoying the calm conditions.

She found Trevallyn House on Harbour Road. It was similar to the other houses except it was slightly bigger, but what it made up for in space it clearly lacked in maintenance. The white paint was cracked in places and one of the shutters on the downstairs window was hanging lopsidedly by its rusty hinge.

She made her way to the front door with flagging spirits but before she could even search for the doorbell, the door opened with a loud creak and a round figure appeared in its frame.

'You must be Dr Hayden, the police doctor from Australia,' Mrs Trevallyn, the elderly guest-house owner, greeted her warmly. 'Welcome to Penhally Bay. I'm sorry things are in such a mess but one of my cleaning girls left me in the lurch a couple of days ago. I haven't found a replacement yet. I'll get Davey to take your luggage upstairs for you. I've put you in room seven. It has the best views of the bay.'

'Er…I actually haven't got my luggage with me just now,' Eloise said with a tiny grimace. 'It's coming…later.'

'Oh well…then,' Mrs Trevallyn smiled cheerily. 'No bother. I expect you'll want to freshen up in any case. There's a bathroom on the landing. You have to be careful with the shower—it can scald you if someone turns a tap on somewhere else.'

Just you wait, Jack Innes, Eloise thought as she made her way up to her room. However, she was pleasantly surprised when she opened the door of room seven. It was quaintly decorated in pink and cream and there was a vase of colourful summer flowers on the dressing-table, the heady fragrance of a single red rose in the centre of the arrangement drawing her like a magnet. She stood in front of the vase, and almost without realising she was doing it she reached out and touched one blood-red velvet petal with her finger. She slowly lifted her hand and looked at the end of her finger, her heart beginning to thud, her hand visibly shaking until she realised there was no trace of blood there.

Eloise stepped back from the flowers and gave herself a mental shake. 'You've been in forensics way too long, my girl,' she said, and went to the window overlooking the bay. She opened it, closed her eyes and breathed in the tangy salty air.

Chief Inspector Lachlan D'Ancey closed the folder with a little snap as he faced his junior colleague. 'I still believe this is going way over the top,' he said. 'I don't see why we need to have an Australian forensic pathologist coming to review something we've already dealt with. We handled this death as we would that any other high-profile person.'

Constable James Derrey gave a little nod of agreement. 'Yes, I know, but apart from the family it looks like someone else down under is asking a lot of questions about the death of this celebrity surfer, Chief. Ethan Jenson was expected to win the World Surfing Championship. The Aussies just don't accept that a surfer of his calibre could accidentally drown. I understand our orders to allow an external case review have come from very high up.'

Lachlan raked a hand through his dark brown, hair making it stick up at irregular angles. 'Yes, they have, but I just hope this forensic pathologist they're sending will see that we've done a first-rate investigation and just go back home and let us get on with doing our job.'

'Yes, sir, I couldn't agree more.'

Lachlan leaned back in his chair with a weary sigh. 'Going through this case file yet again is certainly not my preferred way to spend the next month.'

'Mine neither but this Australian woman will want you present for the whole review to answer questions, no doubt,' James said. 'Have you met her yet?'

Lachlan shook his head and glanced at his watch. 'She was supposed to be here yesterday but maybe something more important cropped up.' He suddenly looked up and grinned as he added, 'Or maybe she got lost. She's probably halfway to Scotland by now. You know what Aussies are like—they drive further for a litre of milk than we do for our annual holidays.'

James smiled back. 'And I bet she has a chip on her shoulder the size of Stonehenge. They always do. Remember that bird that came up from London that time? What is it about career-women anyway?'

There was an awkward little silence.

James had the grace to blush. 'Sorry, Chief,' he mumbled. 'That was in poor taste. I forgot about Margaret and the divorce and all…'

'Forget it, James,' Lachlan said. 'I'm over it. I admit it's been tough, but to tell you the truth we should have split up years ago. In fact, we shouldn't have got married in the first place but Poppy was on the way and, well…' He blew out another sigh and continued, 'I thought it was the right thing to do at the time.'

'How is your daughter?' James asked. 'I heard she was pretty upset about Jenson's death. She was a big fan of his, right?'

Lachlan gave a wry smile. 'You know teenage girls, James, they're all celebrity crazy. There wouldn't be a woman under forty around here who doesn't go weak at the knees when a bronzed surfer with a six pack walks past.'

James got to his feet. 'Yeah, that's true enough. Well, I'd better get back on the job. I've got to check on a possible theft out at Henry Ryall's farm. He thinks some of his sheep are missing but it's more likely he wants some company for a cup of tea. You know what he's been like since Mary died.'

'Poor old chap,' Lachlan said. 'It's probably time he moved closer into town but I don't see that happening in the near future.'

'He'll die with his work boots on for sure,' James agreed. He moved to the door and added, 'Good luck with the forensics lady. You never know, she might be a bit of all right.'

Lachlan didn't answer. He waited until James had left before he opened the file again and looked down at the features of the dead man for a long moment, a small frown bringing his brows closer together…

Eloise found the local police station without too much trouble, although when she opened the front door she was a little surprised there was no one seated at the small front desk. Penhally Bay was so quiet she could hardly believe it had a police station and certainly not one where a chief inspector had been appointed.

She looked over the counter to find a bell or buzzer to push, located a small brass bell and gave it a tinkle. She hovered for another minute or two before she called out, 'Hello? Is anyone there?'

No answer.

She gave the bell another rattle, feeling a little foolish as she did so. But then she had to admit she had never felt more ill prepared for a professional appointment in her life, let alone her first international assignment. It seemed ironic to have been so churned up with nerves only to find the station she had been assigned to work from was far from a high-tech law-enforcement agency.

She was glad now she hadn't wasted precious time trying to find somewhere to buy a new outfit. Somehow turning up in her well-worn jeans and close-fitting vest top with a cotton shirt over the top didn't seem quite so out of place now. Admittedly, there was a coffee stain on her top on her right breast, where the mid-air turbulence had caught both herself and the flight attendant off guard during dinner, and her jeans felt as if they could have stood up all by themselves. As for her face…well…what could she say about her face? At least it was clean—the scalding blast of hot water in the shower a short time ago had not only lifted off thirty-six hours of make-up but what felt like the first layer of skin as well. Her fine blonde hair hadn't appreciated the detergent-like guest-house shampoo, and without her radial brushes and high-wattage hairdryer it was now lying about her scalp like a straw helmet instead of her usual softly styled bob.

She whooshed out a breath and raised her hand to the first door she could find, but before she could place her knuckles on the wood the door suddenly opened and a tall, rock-hard figure cannoned right into her.

'Oh…sorry,' a dark-haired man said as he looked down at her, his strong hands coming down on her arms to hold her upright. 'I didn't realise you were standing there. Did I hurt you?'

Eloise blinked a couple of times, her heart doing a funny little stumbling movement in her chest.

She swallowed and gave herself a mental shake. She was dazed by the sudden contact, that's what it was.

Of course it was, she insisted firmly.

It had nothing to do with intelligent brown eyes the colour of whisky and it had absolutely nothing to do with the feel of male hands on her arms for the first time in…well, a very long time indeed.

'Um…I'm…er…fine….' she said hesitantly. 'I rang the bell

but no one answered. I was just about to knock when you opened the door.'

He gave her a smile that lifted the corners of his mouth, showing even white teeth, except for two on the bottom row that overlapped slightly, giving him a boyish look, even though Eloise calculated he had to be close to forty.

'I'm sorry the front desk is unattended,' he said. 'The constable on duty left on a call half an hour ago and the other constable is off sick. What can I do for you?'

Eloise ran her tongue over her lips in the sort of nervous, uncertain gesture she had thought she had long ago trained herself out of using, but without the armour of her clean-cut business suit and sensible shoes and carefully applied but understated make-up she suddenly felt like a shy teenager.

And it didn't help that he was *so* tall.

She decided she would definitely have to rethink the sensible shoes thing in future otherwise she would be seeing a physiotherapist weekly if she had to crane her neck to maintain eye contact with him all the time. He was six feet one or two at the very least, his shoulders were broad and his skin tanned, as if he made the most of the seaside environment.

'I'm Chief Inspector Lachlan D'Ancey,' he said offering her his hand.

Eloise's stomach did a complicated gymnastics routine as she blinked up at him in surprise.

He was the chief inspector?

Somehow she'd been expecting an overweight, close-to-retirement balding man with a packet a day nicotine habit, not a man who looked like he could run two marathons back to back and not even break a sweat.

Eloise put out her hand to meet his. She was well known back home for her strong, one-of-the-men handshakes, but for some reason this time she couldn't quite pull it off. She felt a faint but unmistakable shiver of reaction shimmy up her spine as his long tanned fingers curled around hers, the slightly calloused feel of his skin against her softness making her feel utterly feminine.

'Er…Eloise Hayden,' she stumbled gauchely. 'Dr Eloise Hayden…from Australia. Sydney, actually. I live there…in the city…near the beach…' *Shut up*, she chided herself. Y*ou're rambling like an idiot.*

One of his dark brows lifted slightly. '*You're* the forensic pathologist?'

Eloise wasn't sure what to make of his tone or his expression. His gaze swept over her again, lingering pointedly on the coffee-stain on her top right over her left breast before returning to meet her eyes.

'Yes,' she answered a little stiffly, removing her hand from his. 'I am.'

A hint of amusement lit his gaze and the edges of his mouth lifted again. 'They must train them very young down under,' he said. 'I was expecting someone much older and with a bit more experience.'

She straightened her spine and eyeballed him as she clipped out, 'I am thirty-two years old and I can assure you I have had plenty of experience.'

This time his expression was far easier to read: it contained a generous measure of mockery. 'Well, then, Dr Hayden from Australia, I hope you will put that experience to good use while you are with us in Penhally Bay,' he said, his lip curling ever so slightly over the words.

Her hands gripped her handbag hanging over her shoulder and her mouth pulled tight as she replied, 'I intend to, Chief Inspector.'

His eyes roved over her again. 'I'm a pretty easygoing chief, but I was expecting someone dressed a little more formally for our first meeting. Or have you been moonlighting in covert operations?'

She lifted her chin, her eyes shooting sparks of livid blue fire at him. 'Actually, I've come straight from an international flight that was delayed for more than twelve hours and my luggage failed to arrive with me—it's probably somewhere over the Middle East by now. So if you have a problem with what I'm wearing, Chief Inspector D'Ancey, perhaps you'd better take it up with my airline, not me.'

Lachlan suppressed an inward smile at her little show of insurgence. She was as Constable Derrey had predicted: a career-woman with a chip on her shoulder, clearly resentful she had to take orders from a man.

She was, however, far more attractive than he had expected in a hard-nosed career-woman. She looked like she could strut along the catwalk with her slim-but-with-curves-in-all-the-right-places figure. Her short chaotic hair was almost but not quite platinum blonde and her eyes a startling clear china blue, in spite of her recent long-haul flight. Her mouth was set in a prim line right now but there was a suspicion of sensuality about it in its soft contours which made him wonder just how much experience she had had and who had enjoyed it with her.

His eyes went to her left hand to see if she was married but her finger was bare. She was wearing a silver watch on her left wrist, an expensive one by the look of it and somewhat at odds with her faded jeans and stained vest top, but he wasn't going to apologise for his comment. Dr Eloise Hayden looked like she needed taking down a peg or two and he was happy to be the one to do it.

'Where are you staying?' he asked.

'Trevallyn House.'

His brows lifted again and his mouth twisted sardonically. 'So your forensics department is cost-cutting, is it?'

Eloise felt like slamming him up against the nearest wall. He was deliberately baiting her, she could tell. She had met so many men like him in her line of work that she had lost count years ago—power hungry, and resentful of a younger woman taking command of an investigation. But she hadn't travelled all this way to be treated like a novice. She had a job to do and woe betide anyone who stood in her way. This was her first international appointment and the success of it would secure her reputation as one of the best forensic pathologists Australia had to offer.

She met his whisky-brown eyes with a level stare even though it made her neck protest. 'I am quite happy with the accommodation I have been assigned,' she said in a curt tone. 'It's right in the centre of the village and I'm used to roughing it whenever necessary.'

'Well you'll certainly be roughing it at Trevallyn House,' he said with a crooked smile. 'Last I heard there was only one toilet working.'

Eloise unclenched her jaw and returned, 'I see no point in wasting taxpayers' money on luxury accommodation when this case could very well go on for longer than first expected.'

Something flickered in his brown gaze as it held hers, but she didn't have time to identify exactly what it was for he masked it so quickly.

'We've done a first-rate investigation, as my briefing showed,' he said. 'I hardly think you will uncover anything that would prolong the investigation any more than a week at the most, no matter how impressive your CV.'

The look she gave him was imperious. 'My review could be straightforward, but there are a few things I do have questions about. I guess that's the whole point of an external review, isn't it? To get a fresh perspective.'

He gave her a cool little smile as he pushed open his office door. 'Let's get started, then,' he said, and indicated for her to precede him inside.

CHAPTER TWO

ELOISE moved past him in the doorway, keeping her arms close to her body in case she inadvertently touched him, but even so the subtle notes of his aftershave drifted towards her, an intoxicating combination of sharp citrus and moody musk that made her nostrils flare involuntarily.

She took the chair opposite his cluttered desk and it was only when she was seated with her legs pressed tightly together that he took his own chair, his brown gaze watchful as it connected with hers.

'So, Dr Hayden,' he began in a seemingly polite tone. 'Was it your choice to come all this way to Penhally Bay or were you the only one available at the time?'

Eloise felt her lips pursing in annoyance. 'There were other people available but my boss thought I had the best mix of skills for this review,' she said. 'It will also be beneficial to my career to take this posting.'

'Is this your first international assignment?' he asked.

'Yes, but that doesn't mean I—'

'This is a small close-knit community,' he interrupted her without apology. 'If you come here with the intention of stirring up a hornet's nest just for the heck of it to score brownie points back home, forget it.'

'I wasn't intending to do any such thing. I just—'

'The autopsy report showed that Ethan Jenson died by drowning,' he cut her off again. 'I doubt very much if you will find out anything more, no matter how talented your boss thinks you are.'

Eloise had trouble containing her anger. She wasn't normally the hot-headed type but something about his manner towards her made her skin start to prickle all over with irritation. She could see what he thought of her in the derisive line of his mouth and the glint of scorn in his gaze every time it came in contact with hers.

She sat up straighter in her chair, her eyes glittering as they held his. 'That was my first question, actually,' she said. 'I'm not happy with the autopsy. The diagnosis of drowning was made mostly on external pathologic findings, but the circumstances of the case don't add up in my mind. How could a world-class surfer drown on a shallow beach? There was only one lung biopsy taken, and that didn't show any oedema. I want to redo the autopsy, and I want more lung tissue and tracheal and bronchial tissue to examine.'

'Are you calling our local pathologist incompetent?' he asked. 'And have you considered the impact of this on the victim's relatives—his mother and father, for instance, or his three younger brothers?'

'I understand that it is a difficult time for the family,' she said. 'But from the autopsy report that I've seen, I could not definitively rule out suicide, or even murder. The finding of accidental death is not conclusive.'

'This is Penhally Bay, not somewhere violent crime is commonplace,' Lachlan said with a heavy frown. 'As far as I'm concerned, the autopsy was carried out by a senior pathologist, the diagnosis was drowning, and there simply were no suspicious circumstances. The closure the family needs right now is to fly their loved one's body home for burial. This has gone on for a week as it is. I see no point in prolonging their agony by performing another autopsy, which will no doubt come up with nothing of significance.'

'But surely you know that the request for another autopsy came via the Jensons' legal advisors in Sydney?' Eloise responded tightly. 'Ethan Jenson had several high-profile sponsors who, along with the family, want firm answers about what happened.'

She snatched in a quick breath and, trying her best not to be intimidated by his laser-like stare, continued, 'You must know yourself the diagnosis of drowning is one of the most difficult in forensic pathology. Sure, there were external signs that the body was in water for some time, but that doesn't mean that death was from drowning. From the report I saw, there was no description of froth in the airway—maybe he was dead first and was then put in the water. The one lung biopsy didn't show emphysema aquosum or pulmonary oedema. And I'm not happy that the diatom test was thorough enough. I want to repeat it on new cardiac, blood, lung, liver, bone marrow and brain tissue, because the diatom report reeks of fresh-water contamination of the samples. And it was qualitative, not quantitative. I want samples of the water at the site where the body was found for a proper comparison.'

Lachlan shifted his lips from side to side as he considered her angle on things. She had made several good points certainly, but he had every faith in the local pathologist and didn't like to rock the boat, so to speak, by openly supporting another autopsy. He understood where the family was coming from in requesting a review of the verdict. A lot of relatives of accidental death victims did the same. It took them time to accept their loved one wasn't coming back. It had only been a week—their pain was still so raw they were still struggling to cope with it all.

'And that brings me to question two,' Eloise said into the taut silence. 'The toxicology results—I noted there was no carbon monoxide assay, yet the victim's hands were noted to be cherry red.'

He returned her direct look with an unblinking stare. 'You're making the autopsy report I received sound completely incompetent, Dr Hayden. I know the pathologist who did the autopsy. He's extremely reliable. I've worked with him many times before. I have the greatest admiration for him.'

'I am sure you do,' she said. 'But no one is perfect and even the best of us miss things at times.'

A corner of his mouth lifted slightly. 'Are you admitting you sometimes get it wrong, Dr Hayden?'

She stared back at him, her lips pulled tight once more. 'Not often but I'm not arrogant enough to assume I never will.'

His mouth was still tilted in a half-smile. 'Let's hope for your sake this is not one of those times, although if what you are telling me is correct, I would have to support a re-examination of the body.'

'Thank you, Chief Inspector D'Ancey,' Eloise said, having trouble concealing the effect his stomach-flipping smile had on her. Every time she looked at him her chest felt as if a tiny moth had landed inside the cage of her lungs and was now fighting for a way out.

She crossed and uncrossed her legs and then added in a businesslike tone, 'And that brings me to question number three. Was Mr Jenson a known drug user?'

'Not that we could ascertain,' he answered as he leaned

back in his chair, his gaze still locked on hers. 'The toxicology report isn't in yet and won't be for another couple of weeks. Why? Do you have additional information on him that we weren't sent?'

'No,' she said, moistening her lips with a darting movement of her tongue. 'I have been given the same files as you have. Ethan Jenson had a couple of DUI charges when he was in his late teens but there has been nothing since. Did you know him personally?'

Lachlan mentally kicked himself for not anticipating her question. He wasn't used to being caught off guard but he had only recently become aware of his daughter's infatuation with the surfer and hadn't yet made up his mind if the rumours currently circulating the village were true. Poppy had admitted she had met the victim on the beach and that he had given her his autograph, but she had denied any other involvement with him, although James Derrey's comment made him wonder if he should have another little private chat with his daughter. But while he knew it wasn't too late for him to be taken off the case, he also knew speculation would increase if he stepped down from the inquiry.

He wondered if Dr Eloise Hayden already suspected something. She had a look of sharp intelligence about her. Those china-blue eyes had been busily assessing him from the word go, her features schooled into cool impassivity while she quietly made up her mind about him.

He leaned back in his chair and idly flicked his pen on and off, the tiny click-clack prolonging the tight-as-a-violin-bow silence.

'As I said a moment ago, Dr Hayden, this is a small close-knit community,' he said. 'The presence of a celebrity surfer in our midst was a big thing. Ethan Jenson was hardly able to walk down the street without someone stopping him for an autograph every few paces.'

'Did you ask him for one?'

He frowned at her. 'No, I did not.'

One of her finely arched brows lifted. 'So you weren't exactly a fan of his, Chief Inspector D'Ancey?'

Lachlan felt like grinding his teeth but somehow he managed to give her a cool smile instead. 'I am usually too busy keeping order in Wadebridge. I have only been assigned this case while you are here as I happen to live locally.'

'I did wonder why someone with your senior ranking would be operating out of such a small community,' she put in. 'Who else is assigned to this station?'

'PC James Derrey and PC Gaye Trembath,' he answered. 'They are the local officers and along with me will help you in any way you require during your stay.'

Eloise privately wondered if Lachlan D'Ancey was going to be more of a help or a hindrance. There was something about his manner that alerted her to an undercurrent of tension running through him. He was good at hiding it, she had to admit, but she'd been working alongside cops long enough to know how much they liked playing their cards close to their chests. He was all cool politeness but behind the screen of his brown eyes was a studied watchfulness that made her suspect he was more than a little uncomfortable with her presence in the village.

Her eyes went to his long-fingered hands, the right one still clicking his pen in that annoying little way that she assumed was meant to intimidate her.

Click. Click. Click. Click.

Her gaze zeroed in on the narrow band of lighter-toned skin of his left hand ring finger, the absence of a ring suggesting he had either lost it recently or that he had been married but was no longer. Somehow she automatically presumed the latter rather than the former. Although his desk was cluttered, everything about him suggested he was an organised and meticulous officer. She couldn't imagine him losing anything or indeed much escaping his notice; he had an aura of quiet but steely authority about him and she couldn't help feeling those whisky-coloured eyes hinted at dark secrets lurking just below the surface.

Her eyes collided with his in the silence, and a sensation like a feather being brushed over the back of her neck made her shift restlessly in her seat again.

'You mentioned your luggage didn't arrive,' he said. 'Is there anything you need for tonight or tomorrow? I can organise some clothes for you. I have a sixteen-year-old daughter who is much the same height and build as you.'

Eloise was surprised at how much his features softened as he spoke of his daughter. The hard set to his mouth relaxed and tender warmth entered his gaze momentarily. He might have been recently separated or divorced from his wife, she thought, but quite clearly not from his offspring.

'That's very kind of you but I'm not sure I will be taken seriously by the locals if I turn up in a sixteen-year-old's attire,' she responded, and after a tiny pause added with a deliberately pointed look, 'I made a bad enough impression on you, turning up in jeans.'

Again a small smile lifted the edges of his mouth. 'Are you expecting an apology from me, Dr Hayden?' he asked.

'No,' she said with a level stare, but her chest cavity started fluttering again. 'But, then, you don't seem the type to hand them out all that frequently.'

He held her look with enviable ease. 'You consider yourself quite good at reading people, don't you?'

There was a tiny almost imperceptible lift of her chin. 'I've hung around cops for a long time, Chief Inspector D'Ancey, so, yes, I am pretty good at it, as I imagine you are too.'

He leaned back in his chair in an indolent manner. 'What do you make of me so far?' he asked.

She pursed her lips for a moment as she considered her reply. 'You like control.'

His expression remained slightly mocking. 'What police officer doesn't?'

'You are also unhappy about me being here to investigate Ethan Jenson's death,' she said, 'but I haven't yet ascertained why.'

His gaze locked on hers again but Eloise couldn't help noticing the way his right thumb began clicking the pen again. 'Maybe I have something against Australians,' he offered dryly.

She tilted her head. 'Or maybe you have something against women—professional women in particular.'

She was good, Lachlan had to hand it to her. She was perceptive but far too attractive for his liking. Not to mention her attitude. She stood up to him in a way few people did, which both intrigued and irritated him.

'I have no problem with career-women as long as they play by the rules,' he said.

'Those would be your rules, I take it?' she put in pertly.

His mouth tightened before he could stop it. 'I am used to being in charge, Dr Hayden,' he said. 'It comes with the title of Chief Inspector. What I say goes.'

'I am here to review the findings of what has been an unexpected death of an Australian citizen,' she said. 'I don't anticipate there being any compromise over protocol. I know how to conduct myself both professionally and personally.'

A taut silence thickened the air for a few pulsing seconds.

'I also know how to deal with difficult colleagues,' she added when he didn't speak.

One of his dark brows lifted. 'You are suggesting I am going to be a difficult colleague?'

She resettled in her chair. 'You are showing all the classic signs of being one.'

His mouth twisted as he held her look. 'And those signs would be?'

Eloise sat silently fuming. Just like so many of the men in the force back home, he was deliberately trying to make her feel inadequate and uncertain. 'You are certainly not what I was expecting,' she said through tight lips.

'And what exactly were you expecting, Dr Hayden from Australia?' he asked. 'A welcoming committee with a brass band and fanfare for your arrival?'

This time Eloise didn't bother disguising her anger. 'No, but the very least I had hoped for was a chief inspector who had an open mind on the case, which clearly you do not. You seem intent on alienating me when hopefully all I will end up doing is to add credence to the results of your own investigation.'

He leaned forward across the desk. 'It seems to me all you are here for is a fast track to promotion,' he ground out. 'This is just the sort of case to do it, isn't it? An Australian celebrity surfer who suddenly turns up dead on Penhally Bay beach.' He leaned back in his chair. 'That could earn you some serious favours with the boss if you raise a whole lot of unsubstantiated allegations and suggest foul play.'

'An alternative finding of possible murder or suicide will be decided on the basis of the results of the fresh autopsy I perform,' she clipped out.

He gave a little snort of derision. 'He'd been in the water for hours. You'd have to be better than good to find anything on him that our guys didn't find, diatoms and airway froth notwithstanding.'

'It never hurts to have an independent review.'

'It never hurts to respect the family either,' he said. 'But apparently you and your superiors have completely missed that angle on things.'

'That's not true,' Eloise said. 'I've already told you it's the family who want to know what really happened to their son and brother. Hugh Jenson, Ethan's father, is an influential person in Australia. He has called in a lot of favours to pull off an uninvited external review of your findings. Surfers do drown, but not usually on calm beaches. The surf report that day noted a meagre one-metre swell, hardly the conditions for a very experienced surfer to drown in.'

His brown gaze became steely. 'Sounds like you've already made up your mind about your review findings. You haven't even examined the body and yet you've reached a conclusion.'

'That's not the case at all,' she insisted. 'I'm trained to keep an open mind, that's imperative in my line of work.'

'Are you, now? Exactly how long have you been a forensic pathologist?' he asked.

Eloise tried to stare him down but it took considerable effort on her part. 'I trained in medicine and then took four years to qualify in general pathology. If you must know, I developed an interest in forensic pathology when I was asked to do histopathology for a string of murders that eventually led to the conviction of a serial killer. I am now employed by the Central Sydney Health Board where I've subspecialised in DNA profiling. Cases that had been cold for ten or more years are now being solved with the new technology. It's meant justice has been served when the victims' families had given up hope of ever finding out what happened.'

'So you're hoping to achieve the same thing for Ethan Jenson's family?' he asked.

'Well, of course,' she answered. 'A review will give them more certainty about what happened to him.'

His gaze bored like a very determined drill into hers. 'What if your trip over here turns out to be a complete and very expensive waste of time?'

Eloise pursed her mouth again. 'I don't see how a second opinion can be a waste of time, Chief Inspector D'Ancey,' she said. 'Or are you worried I might actually prove your local people wrong?'

He held her challenging look. 'Not at all, Dr Hayden,' he said with one of his enigmatic half-smiles. 'I would, however, like you to keep a relatively low profile while you are here. There are many people who have been upset by the death of Ethan Jenson. If you go at it like a bull at a gate, you will hinder any subsequent investigation. The locals will be less likely to co-operate if or when the time comes for our people to interview witnesses.'

Eloise sat back, turning her head slightly to break from his intense gaze.

'I understand from the report faxed to me that Mr Jenson was found at dawn by some local surfers,' she said.

'Yes, he was dead and had been for several hours,' he answered. 'You have a copy of the statements taken individually from the three young men.'

'Where was Mr Jenson staying while he was in town?'

'At one of the pubs—the Penhally Arms. It's on Harbour Road. You would have passed it on your way here.'

'I think I may have seen it,' she said, recalling a blue and white building with colourful baskets of lobelia and petunias hanging outside.

A small silence crept on tiptoe into the room. Eloise wondered if he was deliberately letting it stretch and stretch to make her feel as uncomfortable as possible. She sat up straighter in her chair and trained her eyes on his, although the distinctly audible sound of her stomach rumbling lost her some ground.

Lachlan discreetly cleared his throat and, breaking his gaze, glanced at his watch. 'Oh, is that the time?' he said, and with a forced smile added, 'I'm afraid I'll have to bring our meeting to a close. Duty calls, as they say.'

Eloise got to her feet, not sure if she was being fobbed off or let off the hook. 'That's fine. I have to go too. We've gone way past our scheduled half-hour. I want to introduce myself at the medical clinic.'

'Why's that?' he asked, frowning slightly. 'You'll be based here.'

'I realise that but your report indicated one of the local doctors…' she glanced down at her notes to check the doctor's name '…Nick Tremayne, was called to the scene. I have some questions about his examination of the body, that's all. Where will I be working from here?' Eloise asked glancing pointedly around the cramped office. 'This seems a rather small station.'

'It is,' he answered, 'but we've assigned you a small office out the back. If it proves inadequate, arrangements can be made for you to travel back and forth to the main station at Wadebridge.'

'I'll probably move between the two,' she said. 'I wouldn't want to get under anyone's feet.' *Or at least not yours*, she thought.

'I'll show you the way to the clinic,' he said, and came from behind his desk, hooking his jacket off the chair with one finger.

'There's really no need,' she said. 'I can find it myself. Mrs Trevallyn at the guest-house gave me a tourist map.'

'It's fine,' he said holding the door open for her. 'I'm heading that way myself.'

Eloise moved past him in the doorway, this time not quite managing to keep from touching him. It was the briefest brush of her arm against his but it was enough to send a shock wave of reaction right through her body.

Careful, she reminded herself sternly as she followed him outside. Mixing business and pleasure had never worked for her in the past and she had sworn after what had happened with Bill Canterbury that she'd never be tempted to do it again.

And she hadn't been, not even once.

Until now…

CHAPTER THREE

'THAT offer of a change of clothes is still on if you change your mind,' Lachlan said as he led the way to the clinic. 'There are a few shops locally but they probably won't have much more than T-shirts, swimsuits and sarongs at this time of year.'

Eloise bit her lip as she thought about how she was going to cope without her luggage. She needed a toothbrush and a change of underwear at the very least. She could probably spin another day out in her jeans but the vest top *had* to go.

'I'm sure Poppy won't mind,' he added. 'She's got too many clothes as it is. I'm forever picking them up off the floor.'

She gave him a sideways glance. 'I wouldn't like to put her out or anything. Perhaps you should ask her first to see if it's all right.'

He suddenly frowned as he looked towards the clinic entrance. 'Looks like you can ask her yourself,' he said.

Eloise followed the line of his gaze and saw a beautiful-looking girl with long blonde hair coming towards them. She was tanned and slim, her brown eyes made up with smoky eye-shadow and eyeliner making her look much older than sixteen. She had a rather serious look on her face, and in spite of the carefully applied eye-make up Eloise suspected she had been crying recently, but as soon as the girl saw her father her expression turned from serious to surly.

'I thought you were working until seven tonight,' she said, and then with a quick glance at Eloise turned back to her father, her mouth twisting sarcastically. 'What's going on? Are you arresting her or dating her?'

Lachlan opened his mouth to reprimand his daughter but Eloise got in first. She gave the girl a polite but distinctly cool smile and introduced herself. 'Hello, Poppy, I'm Eloise Hayden. I'm afraid I've come to ask a favour of you.'

Poppy looked a little startled, making her look more like a small child instead of an in-your-face teenager. 'You...you have?' she croaked.

'Dr Hayden's luggage has gone missing,' Lachlan explained before Eloise could get another word in. 'I thought you might be able to tide her over for a couple of days with something out of your extensive wardrobe.'

This time the young girl's expression changed from frowning worry to a sneer. 'I hardly think anything of mine will fit her,' she said, folding her arms across her chest. 'She's much bigger than me.'

Catty little girl, Eloise thought behind the screen of her deadpan expression, although she automatically sucked in her tummy and wished not for the first time that she hadn't inherited her mother's generous breasts.

'She's got a beautiful figure, just like you,' Lachlan growled. 'Now, stop being so appallingly rude to her.'

You're a fine one to talk, Eloise would have been tempted to say normally, but she was still reeling from his assessment of her figure as beautiful.

Poppy's lip curled. 'So you *are* dating her, then, are you?'

'Er...no,' Eloise said quickly, hating it that she was

blushing and that Lachlan was witnessing every agonising second of it. 'I'm here on official business.'

The worried frown came back. 'Is it something to do with Ethan Jenson?' Poppy asked.

'Yes,' Eloise said. 'I'm a forensic pathologist from Australia, appointed to review the investigation into his death.'

Poppy's brown gaze flicked to her father's. 'I thought it was already sorted out—you know, that he drowned and no one else was responsible.'

'Dr Hayden will no doubt come to the same conclusion,' he said with a challenging little glint in his eyes as he looked at Eloise.

Eloise gritted her teeth and turned back to his daughter. 'Did you know him, Poppy?' she asked.

The girl's eyes fell away from hers. 'Not really,' she mumbled. 'I met him once or twice but that was ages ago.'

'Ages ago when?'

'Dr Hayden, this is neither the time nor place to conduct an interview with my daughter even if you were authorised to do so,' Lachlan said firmly. 'Come on, Poppy, we have an appointment, remember?'

Poppy looked confused. 'We do?'

'Yes. You asked me to take you to Fiona's place.'

'But that's tomor—'

'We'll leave some clothes for you at the guest-house,' Lachlan said to Eloise as he ushered his daughter away with a firm hand at her elbow.

Eloise stood watching them until they disappeared around the corner. Chief Inspector D'Ancey quite clearly didn't want her talking even casually to his daughter about Ethan Jenson, which made her wonder if the girl had been lying about how well she had known the surfer.

'Are you looking for somebody?' a female voice said from behind her.

Eloise turned to see an elegant-looking woman in her mid to late forties standing at the entrance to the medical clinic. 'Oh, yes, sorry I was just coming in to introduce myself,' she said. 'I'm Eloise Hayden from Australia, I'm here to—'

'We've been expecting you,' the woman said with a warm smile. 'I'm Kate Althorp, one of the midwives here. Come inside and I'll introduce you to the practice manager, Hazel, and Sue, the head receptionist. Dr Tremayne is with a patient but he'll be out shortly. I'm afraid the other doctors have either left for the day or are out on calls, but you will probably meet them over the next few days.'

Eloise followed the woman inside the two-storey building, taking in with interest the comfortable-looking waiting room with a children's play area in one corner and the neat reception area on the left.

After exchanging greetings from the two women behind the reception desk, Kate looked up as a tall man with dark hair peppered with grey came out of the first room off the waiting area.

'Ah here's Dr Tremayne now,' she said. 'Nick, this is Eloise Hayden, the forensics specialist from Australia.'

'How do you do?' Nick said, offering Eloise his hand for the briefest of handshakes. 'Welcome to Penhally Bay.'

'Thank you,' Eloise said. 'I was wondering if I could ask you some questions about Ethan Jenson. You were the one who examined him at the scene, I understand?'

'Yes,' he answered somewhat brusquely.

'Is now a convenient time, or can we make another time soon?' Eloise asked. 'It won't take too long if you've got a minute or two available.'

His brows moved closer together. 'I am extremely pushed at the moment,' he said. 'I still have a house call to make.'

'Mrs Griggs won't mind waiting for you,' Kate interjected. 'She understands when you get caught up.'

Nick Tremayne exchanged a quick glance with Kate before turning back to Eloise. 'Come through to my room,' he said. 'But it will have to be quick.'

Eloise followed him into his consulting room, sat in one of the two chairs available and quietly observed him. She couldn't help noticing he seemed on edge and impatient as he took his seat.

'Right, fire away,' he said, folding his arms.

'Was the body still in the water when you were called?' she asked.

'No,' he answered. 'The deceased had been dragged onto the beach by the three boys who had found him.'

'So how long after he had been removed from the water did you see the body, Dr Tremayne?'

'The body was found at six a.m. and I saw him around seven-thirty so it was about an hour and a half.'

'Was the body covered by anything in that time?' she asked.

'Yes,' he said. 'When I arrived a blanket had been placed over the body as there were quite a few people gathering on the beach at that time.'

'Do you remember what type of blanket, what colour, what it was made of?' Eloise asked.

'Wool, I think…brown, if I remember correctly.' His deep brown gaze narrowed slightly as it returned to hers. 'Is there some query about my assessment of the body?'

'No, there's no specific query about your assessment at all,' she said. 'It's just that there are some aspects of the case that are puzzling, and I'm just trying to clear them up. The

Australian authorities have been invited to carry out an external review of the death. There's no question of competence—more a fresh look to see if anything surfaces that might not have come to light so far.'

Eloise waited a beat or two and when he didn't respond, she continued, 'So he'd been out of the water for one and a half hours before you saw him and you are quoted as saying at the time you thought he had drowned. Can you tell me what made you so sure that drowning was the actual cause of his death? Could he have died from another cause and been placed in the water later?'

His brows moved together. 'Murdered, you mean?'

'It happens in the quietest villages as well as the biggest cities, Dr Tremayne.'

He held her direct look. 'There were no other obvious causes for his death. He had no external marks of trauma. He was in the water and as far as I could see he had drowned. I believe the autopsy bore out my assessment.'

'It did, yes. But, still, there are a couple of features I need to clarify.'

'Such as?'

'Well, for one, I notice in your statement that the hands and feet were somewhat pinkish—that's not quite consistent with the cyanosis you would expect after a drowning. Also, the deceased was a world-class swimmer and the ocean swell was relatively calm that morning. Why would someone who has faced some of the world's most challenging waves drown on a calm beach?'

'Surfers do occasionally drown,' he pointed out. 'They're human, like everyone else. They're not immune to freakish accidents.'

'Yes, but if Ethan Jenson had met with an accident of some

sort, one would expect to see some sign of it on his body—a head wound, for instance, if his surfboard had rendered him unconscious, but your report did not identify any such signs of injury or trauma.'

'That is because there weren't any,' he stated with an air of impatience as he glanced at his watch. 'The pathologist, Peter Middleton, didn't find any either.'

Eloise held her ground and continued, 'I'm not actually all that happy with some of the tests done at the autopsy—some of them were not as complete as I would have liked, and there were a couple of tests I would like to have seen done which weren't.'

He frowned darkly. 'Has another autopsy been authorised?'

'Yes. His family, along with his sponsors, requested it via their lawyers. The coroner has been informed and I've been given the go-ahead.'

'That's going to delay getting this matter cleared up, isn't it?' he commented, still frowning slightly. 'Still, you're the forensic specialist, Dr Hayden. I wish you well in clearing up your doubts. But as far as I can ascertain, the victim looked as though he went to the beach for an early morning swim and for some reason got into difficulties and drowned. I'm no Sherlock Holmes, but that was my clinical assessment and that's what the local pathologist decided was the case. Now, I really must be off. If I can be of further assistance, Hazel or Sue will make an appointment for you to see me.'

'Thank you for your time,' Eloise said, and got to her feet.

Kate caught up with Eloise once Nick had stalked out of the practice, mumbling something to the receptionist on his way past. 'Don't take his offhand manner personally,' she said with an expressive roll of her eyes. 'He's like that with everyone.'

'This village seems to have its fair share of difficult men,' Eloise remarked with wryness.

Kate gave her a speculative look. 'So you and the chief inspector didn't quite hit it off? I saw you together earlier.'

'I'm not here to make friends but to find out the truth about a young man's death,' Eloise said firmly.

'Lachlan D'Ancey is a pillar of this community,' Kate said as she walked Eloise to the front entrance. 'I'm sure you'll change your opinion of him when you spend more time with him. Nick, however, is another story. I've known him a long time and he's as arrogant and aloof as ever.'

Eloise couldn't help feeling there was a hint of regret in the other woman's tone. Kate Althorp carried herself with natural elegance, but every now and again her warm brown eyes seemed sad, as if life had not turned out quite the way she had hoped. 'There are three other doctors here, aren't there?' she said. 'Including Dr Tremayne's son, Edward.'

'Yes, he's just got married and he's on his honeymoon at the moment,' Kate answered. 'But with the workload increasing all the time, we're taking on a new doctor, Oliver Fawkner, in a week or two. We also have two nurses, Gemma and Alison.'

'It sounds like a busy practice,' Eloise offered.

'It is,' Kate said. 'The closest hospital is St Piran, half an hour away, so we service quite a large area, although I imagine not as large an area as some places in your country.'

'Yes, indeed,' Eloise agreed. 'Before I specialized, I did a short locum in the outback where we had to fly everywhere to see patients on remote cattle stations. It was certainly very different from working in the city.'

'Has anyone come over with you?' Kate asked once they were outside. 'A partner or your husband perhaps?'

'No,' Eloise answered with a rueful look. 'I'm not currently attached. I guess I've been too busy concentrating on my career.'

'It's a lonely life without a partner to share the highs and lows. I should know—I lost my husband some years ago.' She let out a little sigh and added, 'A rescue went horribly wrong during a storm. I lost James and Nick lost his father and brother. It was a terrible time.'

'I'm so sorry,' Eloise said, 'how very tragic for you all.'

'I have a son Jem, short for Jeremiah,' Kate said with a smile of maternal tenderness. 'I don't know how I would have survived without him.'

'Have you lived most of your life in Penhally Bay?'

'Yes,' Kate said. 'I trained as a midwife but after James died I felt I needed a change and sort of drifted into administration and eventually became Practice Manager here. But I went back to midwifery, which is my first love.'

'How old is your son?' Eloise asked.

'He's just turned nine,' Kate answered, and with a wistful smile added, 'Still a little boy but not for much longer, I expect…'

'It must be a lovely place to bring up a child,' Eloise said as the breeze brought the salty tang of the sea towards them. She glanced out of the open window and looked at the wide view of the sparkling blue of Penhally Bay below. 'I read in one of the tourist brochures that there's a seventeenth-century Spanish wreck in the bay and smugglers' caves. That would hold considerable appeal for many a young boy, I imagine.'

'Yes…' Kate said, her expression gradually becoming sombre again. 'I really feel for Mr and Mrs Jenson. They were here yesterday. Nick spent over an hour with them. I can't imagine the hell they're going through, wondering if their son was murdered or committed suicide.'

'So you don't think he just drowned?' Eloise asked, phrasing her question carefully.

Kate's creased brow indicated she hadn't quite made up her mind. 'It's hard to say,' she said after a little pause as she looked out over the bay before turning back to face Eloise. 'He was a brilliant surfer—some say he had the potential to be one of the best ever. My son showed me a photo in a surfing magazine of Ethan riding at Shipstern's Bluff in Tasmania, reputedly the largest and most dangerous waves in the southern hemisphere. Like his family, I find it hard to believe he could come to Penhally Bay in Cornwall and drown. It doesn't make sense.'

'The local authorities seem convinced otherwise,' Eloise returned before she could check herself, 'Chief Inspector D'Ancey in particular. He seems to think my presence here is only going to make things worse for the grieving relatives.'

Kate frowned. 'Yes, there is that, I suppose, but if it had been my son I would want to know for sure what had happened to him. What if it *was* foul play?'

'Was he popular amongst the locals?' Eloise asked.

'He was *very* popular with the girls,' Kate said. 'I guess that might have annoyed some of the local lads a bit, but not enough for anyone to want to get rid of him, I wouldn't have thought.'

'What about his surfing rivals?'

Kate pressed her lips together for a moment. 'I guess if someone wanted to win the next surfing round enough, they might be tempted to eradicate the running favourite, but unlike some sports, where fans take their allegiance to extremes, the surfers all know each other very well and any rivalry is generally friendly.'

Eloise knew she was probably overstepping her professional boundaries but she didn't see the harm in getting some background on the victim and how he had been accepted in the village. 'So you can't think of anyone who would want Ethan Jenson dead?' she asked.

After a brief pause Kate met her questioning gaze levelly. 'There are probably dozens of fathers of teenage girls in the district who are secretly glad Ethan Jenson is out of the way. He had a bit of reputation, if you know what I mean.'

'So he was a bit of a player locally?'

'Very much so,' Kate answered. 'But it comes with the celebrity status, doesn't it? Mind you, young women these days seem to want to play around just as much as the men. They crow about which high-profile person they've bedded and how often. Times have certainly changed.'

'Yes, they have,' Eloise said, thinking of her staid and conservative foster-parents' views on dating.

'Where are you staying while you are here?' Kate asked.

'Trevallyn House. It seems very comfortable and close to everything.'

'Beatrice Trevallyn is a real sweetheart,' Kate said with a soft smile. 'She'll make sure you're well fed and her son is quite a character. He's got learning difficulties but he's lovely. You'll often see him about the village, doing odd jobs for people. Bea's done a good job keeping things going as long as she has since she lost her husband. The place is a bit run down and could do with a lick of paint but I don't think she has the money to do it. She'll be tickled pink you've chosen to stay there.'

'She's made me very welcome,' Eloise said. 'She gave me a lovely room overlooking the bay.'

'How long are you staying in Penhally Bay?' Kate asked.

'I've been assigned a month but it depends on whether I find anything that changes the verdict on Mr Jenson's death. If that should be the case, I would be called on to give evidence if there's an inquest or trial.'

'What the poor Jensons need to do is lay their son to rest,' Kate said with another sombre look.

'I understand how difficult it is for them at a time like this,' Eloise said. 'I've been involved in other cases that dragged on for several weeks in order to identify the bodies of victims after a bomb attack or fire. It's hard on everyone.'

Kate grimaced. 'I don't know how you do it, handling dead bodies all the time. I still struggle to hold myself together when we have a stillborn. I have to be strong for the parents but inside I feel nearly as devastated as they do.'

'I've had to toughen up a lot,' Eloise admitted. 'After my first autopsy I didn't eat meat for a year. I still can recall the smells of my first murder scene. But it's worth it to see justice served. The families can at least draw some measure of comfort that the person or persons responsible are locked away for good or for a very long time.'

'The chief inspector's not long ago gone through a drawn-out and particularly harrowing divorce,' Kate said. 'I think he might be finding being a single dad of a sixteen-year-old daughter quite a steep learning curve. Poppy's a bit of a handful, she's at that difficult age. All hormones and moods and missing her mother, no doubt, although she'd never admit to it, of course.'

'Did you know the chief inspector's ex-wife well?' Eloise asked, with what she hoped sounded like mild interest.

'Margaret D'Ancey didn't have much time for the locals,' Kate said. 'Or at least not since she was promoted in the financial investment firm she works for in London. I often wondered why she got married in the first place—a career always seemed to be more important to her than her husband and daughter. She was always leaving Lachlan to look after Poppy while she went off to some high-powered seminar. I don't know how he managed to juggle it all, given the stresses and strains of his job.'

Eloise found it difficult to know what to say in response. She valued her career above everything else in her life so far. Marriage and babies was something she tried not to think about too much. Years of dealing with crime and death had made her realise how tenuous life really was. The thought of bringing a child into the world only to lose it through an accident or a random act of murder was so terrifying she had more or less ruled it out as an option for her life. Besides, no one had entered her life who she had felt she could spend the rest of her days with. Her forensics colleague Bill Canterbury had been the closest she'd come to considering the possibility, but the fallout from their brief interaction had taught her to keep her private life separate from her professional life. She hadn't been in love with anyone so far, or at least not the sort of love that novels and movies portrayed as permanently life-changing. She wondered, given her background, if she ever would trust anyone enough to love them.

Kate gave her a searching look. 'I hope I didn't offend you. You've gone very silent. I didn't mean to suggest there's anything wrong with having a career or anything.'

'No, of course you didn't offend me,' Eloise said with a re-assuring smile. 'My career is a high priority at the moment but that's not to say it will always be so, although to be honest I don't really have any great desire to settle down right now.'

'You don't want children at some point?' Kate asked.

'I've thought about it once or twice but I haven't met a man I respect and trust enough to be the father of my child,' Eloise said truthfully. 'Most of the women I know are doing it single-handedly, having been deserted and left holding the baby, so to speak. Their chances of finding a new partner are pretty bleak with a couple of kids in tow. It looks like too much hard work if you ask me.'

'I know,' Kate said with a rueful look. 'A lot of men don't want the baggage of another man's child. Besides, it's hard on young kids, having people come and go in their life. I want my son to feel secure, it's so important at his age.'

'It's important at any age,' Eloise said, thinking of her various stints in foster-care after her mother had died of a drug overdose. It had taken years for her to settle down with June and Charles Roberts, and even now she still wondered if they had regretted their decision to parent the nine-year-old daughter of a heroin-addicted prostitute and a father registered as unknown.

Kate glanced at her watch. 'I have to get going—Jem will be wondering what's happened to me. Is there anything you need from the clinic or will you just be interviewing Nick?'

'Thanks, but I think Chief Inspector D'Ancey's organised all the equipment I'll need at the station at Wadebridge. I'll be performing the autopsy tomorrow and will then have to process some tests in the lab—the results may take a few days. Normally they take several weeks but this is a high-profile case so it will be given top priority.'

'It's still all a bit of a waiting game, though, isn't it?' Kate said.

Eloise let out a little sigh. 'Yes, it is, but that's life, right?'

Kate's small world-weary smile seemed to say it all. 'Yes, it certainly is.'

CHAPTER FOUR

'DR HAYDEN, there's a bag of things for you here,' Beatrice Trevallyn said as Eloise came downstairs later that evening. 'Chief Inspector D'Ancey dropped them off a few minutes ago. I asked him if he wanted to see you but he seemed in a bit of a hurry. I expect it's that daughter of his,' she tut-tutted, and added, 'That Poppy is going to be trouble, I can tell. She's far too grown up for her age. If she's not careful she'll have the reputation of Molly Beale.'

Eloise was inclined to agree with Mrs Trevallyn on what she had seen so far of Lachlan D'Ancey's daughter. Poppy certainly wouldn't be an easy teenager to manage. She came across as street-wise and moody. She also had the body of a woman, even though she was little more than a child. The chief inspector would have his work cut out for him, keeping some semblance of control, she imagined, especially without the close back-up of the girl's mother.

She took the carrier bag from the elderly lady's hands and asked, 'Who is Molly Beale?'

Beatrice's mouth was pulled tight. 'My cleaning girl—you know, the one I told you left me without notice? I let her have one of my rooms on the cheap because her mother kicked her out when she got a new man herself, but I wish I hadn't now. Molly was no better than she should have been, if you know what I mean.'

'Have you found someone else to help you in the house?' Eloise asked, out of politeness rather than any real interest.

'I'm interviewing a couple of women tomorrow,' Beatrice said, and then glancing around to see if any of the other guests were within earshot she said in an undertone, 'Davey saw them together, you know, down at the beach.'

Eloise found herself whispering back. 'Saw who?'

'That man that was drowned,' Beatrice said with an air of puffed-up authority. 'It wasn't the first time either. Poppy D'Ancey was seeing him behind Robert Polgrean's back.'

Eloise could feel her intrigue building. 'Who is Robert Polgrean?' she asked.

'Her boyfriend,' Beatrice answered. 'Or at least he was until that surfer came to town and lured her away from him. Robert was devastated and still is, mind you. He and Poppy had been going out since their first year at secondary school.'

'Sixteen is rather young to be thinking of permanency in a relationship,' Eloise felt obliged to say in the girl's defence. 'Kids of that age fall in and out of love almost weekly.'

Beatrice's bird-like eyes narrowed disapprovingly. 'And in and out of bed almost daily, if what Davey saw is to be believed. That girl has been running amok since her mother left. Of course, the chief inspector does his best but he's got to work full time to provide for her, doesn't he? Margaret should have stayed at home and been a proper mother to the girl, instead of gallivanting off, trying to prove how clever she is.'

Eloise had to bite her tongue to stop herself launching into one of her well-used feminist soapbox speeches. She suspected that, like her conservative foster-parents Beatrice wouldn't be all that impressed with her line of argument.

Instead, she tactfully changed the subject. 'I thought I might go out for a walk along the bay. I've got my key with me so don't wait up.'

'It's a lovely evening,' Beatrice said. 'If I wasn't so troubled with my rheumatism, I'd join you. It's been many a long year since I've been able to get down to the water. But it's a fair walk to the surf beach.'

'I love walking and I live near the beach at home,' Eloise said. 'I never really feel my day is complete unless I dip my toes in.'

One of the other guests came down the stairs at that moment and Beatrice turned to speak to them. 'Good evening, Mr Price. Do you fancy a cup of tea or are you on your way out?'

'A cup of tea would be absolutely marvellous, thank you,' a man in his early seventies said with an interested glance in Eloise's direction.

'This is Dr Hayden from Australia,' Beatrice said. 'She's investigating the death of the surfer.'

The man's bushy grey brows rose over his faded blue eyes. 'Oh, really?'

Eloise smiled politely. 'I'm pleased to meet you, Mr Price. Are you holidaying in the area?'

'Yes and no,' he answered with a somewhat quirky smile. 'I'm a writer. I take my work with me wherever I go.'

'Mr Price writes crime fiction, don't you, Mr Price?' Beatrice said.

'Yes,' he said, still smiling.

'Mr Price comes here every year, don't you, Mr Price?' Beatrice said with a fond look.

'I do indeed,' he answered. 'I love the sea air and Mrs Trevallyn's Cornish pasties. They are the best I've ever tasted.'

Eloise hadn't heard of him but, then, she'd never been much of a crime fiction fan, and even less so since she'd been working in forensics. The thought of reading about the sort of stuff she dealt with on a daily basis was not exactly her idea of relaxation, but she didn't like to burst the man's bubble too brutally. 'I look forward to reading one of your books soon,' she said with another polite smile.

Mr Price gave her a sheepish look. 'Um…I'm not actually published just yet but I have a manuscript with an agent in New York as we speak.'

'Isn't that exciting?' Beatrice's round cheeks glowed. 'We'll be able to say we knew Mr Price before he became famous.'

'I also have another manuscript I'm working on with me upstairs.' Mr Price smiled at Eloise. 'I know it's probably a dreadful imposition on my part, but if you had time, would you mind reading the first couple of chapters for me to see if I've got the police procedure right?'

'I'm not sure if I'm the right person to help you,' Eloise said, relieved she had thought of a valid excuse in time. 'Even though I'm called a police surgeon, I'm not really a police officer. I'm employed by the Health Department. Besides, the police have different ways of doing things in Australia. They even call their officers of the same rank different names.'

Mr Price began to beam from ear to ear. 'But my work in progress is set in Australia, in the outback actually, and the main character is a forensic doctor. Isn't that fortuitous?'

Eloise felt like rolling her eyes. Instead, she smiled a smile that felt like it had been stitched to her face with fencing wire. 'In that case, Mr Price, I'd be happy to look over it— perhaps Mrs Trevallyn could drop it into my room,' she said. Excusing herself, she made her way back upstairs with the carrier bag Lachlan D'Ancey had left for her.

Once in the privacy of her room she took out the various items of clothing and laid them on the bed, grimacing ruefully as she thought of her neutral coloured, businesslike skirts and jackets still in transit somewhere between Cornwall and Sydney.

She picked up a brightly flowery patterned skirt and matching sleeveless top and absently rubbed the silky fabric between her fingers, her thoughts automatically drifting to the last time she had seen her mother. She could still remember the garish colour of her mother's silk dress that day, and the cloying scent of her perfume, and the way her mouth had been a red slash of lipstick, the end of a cigarette jutting out from her lips as she'd mumbled something about being a good girl while Mummy went to work.

Eloise let the fabric drop to the bed and, turning on her heel, left the room and the ghosts she'd summoned locked safely inside.

Eloise saw Lachlan D'Ancey as soon as she walked past the café on Harbour Road. He was standing talking to a local fisherman, the smile on his face easy and relaxed, his casual jeans and black polo shirt taking nothing away from his naturally commanding presence.

He looked up and locked gazes with her and then, turning back to his companion, politely excused himself and sauntered over. 'Out for an evening stroll, Dr Hayden?' he asked.

'Yes,' she said. 'But I'm glad I ran into you as I have a couple of questions for you.'

'Professional or personal?'

'A bit of both, actually.'

If her answer rattled him he showed no sign of it. His face remained an indifferent mask as he held her gaze. 'I suppose back home you would be just starting work for the day,' he commented as he glanced momentarily at his watch. 'Or are you so career focused that you work around the clock?'

She gave him a brittle look. 'If the case calls for it, I put in whatever hours are necessary.'

'You know what they say about all work and no play, Dr Hayden,' he said with a teasing glint in his eyes.

Eloise lifted her chin. 'And you know what they say about people getting away with murder, Chief Inspector.'

The corners of his mouth lifted. 'What *do* they say, Dr Hayden?' he asked.

Eloise felt a hot little spark of attraction set fire to her insides. She could feel the flames slowly but inexorably spreading, heating her in every secret place. Her breasts felt tight and tender, her mouth felt dry and her heart felt as if it had forgotten its normal rhythm entirely. She sent the tip of her tongue out to run over the surface of her lips, her stomach feeling as if a miniature pony had begun kicking inside her as Lachlan's lazy brown gaze followed the path of her tongue.

She tried to drag her mushy brain back to the conversation at hand. 'Um…'

He cocked one brow in enquiry. 'Um?'

She moistened her mouth again. 'I forgot what we were talking about…'

'We were talking about people getting away with murder.'

'Oh… Yes…' She looked down at the map in her hands to escape the slow burn of his gaze. 'I was hoping to have a look at the place where the body was found. Could you point me in the right direction?'

'I'll come with you,' he said, and led the way down Harbour Road towards a church that was situated above the lighthouse.

He glanced down at her flat but thinly strapped sandals after a moment or two. 'Will you be all right on the steps down to the beach in those?'

'Of course,' Eloise said, hoping he couldn't see the blister on her left little toe that was growing bigger by the minute.

The swell was rough, with dumping waves stirred by the stiff onshore breeze. She pushed her hair back out of her eyes and soldiered on, stopping when he did at the edge of the foamy waterline.

'He was found floating out there,' he said, pointing to just beyond the first breakers.

Eloise stepped closer so she could follow the line of his arm, her nostrils widening as she smelt his freshly showered smell.

'I've organised some new water samples for you,' he added. 'They'll be at the lab tomorrow.'

Eloise looked out at the rolling ocean and wondered yet again what circumstances had led to the surfer's death. Dr Tremayne was right in saying surfers were not immune to drowning, but she still felt something was not quite right about the way the case had been handled, especially since Ethan Jenson had been a celebrity. As far as she understood it from her experience back home, the normal protocol on high-profile people was extensive testing on autopsy and yet only the most basic tests had been performed. It was a sensitive process: by coming here she would be at risk of offending the local pathologist, questioning his verdict, and yet she felt compelled to leave no stone unturned no matter what egos were dented in the process.

She was still deep in thought when she felt Lachlan's hands suddenly grasp her upper arms. 'What the—*Oh!*'

The foamy water of a larger wave caught her off guard and in spite of his attempts to get her out of the way, her feet and ankles were soaked, her jeans clinging damply to her lower legs.

'Sorry, I should have warned you earlier,' he said with a wry grimace. 'It got me, too.'

She looked down at his feet but, being so much taller, the water had barely come over the top of his shoes.

'Do you want to take your sandals off?' he asked.

Eloise knew that if she took them off she'd never be able to put them on again with that blister throbbing the way it was. 'No, they'll dry on the way back,' she said, and trudged on.

Lachlan walked alongside her, his fingers still feeling the tiny electric aftershocks of touching her bare arms as he'd pulled her out of the wave's way. He made a determined effort not to brush his shoulders against hers each time they came upon one of the narrow sections of the pathway, but he felt the magnetic pull of her all the same.

He was quite surprised to realise he quite liked her take-no-prisoners attitude. For, unlike his ex-wife who had ridden roughshod over everyone she could to get to where she wanted to go, Eloise's brusque, businesslike attitude was looking more and more like a façade. He saw it now and again when she thought he wasn't looking. A shadow of uncertainty would flicker in her eyes, like a gull suddenly flying past the sun, momentarily blocking the light.

'You're limping,' he said as they came back to the start of Harbour Road.

Her chin went up and she straightened her shoulders. 'No, I'm not.'

Lachlan suppressed a little smile. *There, what did I tell you? Nothing but a façade.*

Eloise stiffened when he bent down in front of her and began to inspect her feet. She scrunched up her toes, hoping it would hide the evidence, but it seemed he hadn't been appointed Chief Inspector for nothing.

'You've got a blister,' he said. 'I can see it.' His finger

brushed ever so gently against her foot, sending a jolt of awareness right up her leg.

Eloise looked down at his head, which was at her waist height, and her stomach gave a flustered little quiver. He had such thick, dark wavy hair that her fingers ached to feel its springiness. 'I—It's nothing. I can hardly feel it…'

He straightened and locked gazes with her. 'Do you fancy a drink?' he asked after a tiny pause.

Eloise stared up at him wide-eyed, her mouth opening and closing, although no sound came out.

He suddenly grinned. 'You're looking at me as if I've just asked you to swim the English Channel.'

His gaze shifted from hers to look back at the ocean for a moment. 'Have you got someone back home waiting for you?' he asked.

'No.' Eloise immediately wished she hadn't been so quick to answer. Even in such a liberated age there were few women over the age of thirty who liked admitting they were without a partner. 'Not at present,' she added lamely.

He turned and gave her a speculative look. 'So, like me, you're in between relationships.'

'Sort of…I guess.'

'So there'd be no harm in having a drink now that we both know where we stand,' he said. 'Besides, you need to rest your foot for a while. That blister looks painful. What do you say?'

She examined his expression guardedly. 'I wouldn't want you to get the wrong idea…'

His smile was crooked and Eloise thought perhaps a little self-deprecating. 'You're going to have to help me out here, Dr Hayden,' he said. 'It's been years since I asked a woman out for a drink. If you refuse my very first attempt, it might permanently damage my ego and you know what they say about the fragility of the male ego.'

Eloise made a little moue with her lips. 'Yes, but I've never had cause to believe it was true,' she said, still trying not to smile. 'Anyway, I'm sure your ego will bounce back quite rapidly and robustly if I say no.'

His brown eyes gleamed. 'You said *if*, so does that mean I'm still in with a chance?' he asked.

Eloise felt herself wavering, even though she wondered if his rather endearing desperate and dateless act was exactly that—just an act. But she reasoned a drink at one of the nearby pubs was a good way to get a feel for the local area, perhaps even meet a few of the regulars.

She blew out a little sigh. 'All right,' she said. 'One drink but one drink only.'

He stood looking down at her with that lopsided boyish smile of his. 'Tell me something, Dr Hayden from Australia. When was the last time you were asked out for a drink by a man?' he asked.

Eloise hated it that she had to really think about it before answering.

Had it been *that* long?

'Um…a few months,' she said. Two years more like, but she wasn't going to admit that to him.

He paused and then smiled again, liking the fact that he was getting to see a little bit of the real Eloise Hayden.

'What about a kiss?'

She gave him a wary look. 'What about a kiss?'

His smile was still tilting up one side of his mouth. 'Have you been kissed by a man in the last few months?'

'Of course,' she said, thinking of the slightly embarrassed peck on the cheek she had received from her foster-father at the airport.

Reaching for one of her hands and securing it in the warmth of his, Lachlan asked, 'How many months?'

She gave him a back-off stare but for some reason couldn't quite summon up the strength to counteract his gentle but firm hold. 'I don't see that it's any of your business.'

He shrugged. 'What if I said I'm making it my business? I'm interested in getting to know you, Dr Hayden,' he said, his fingers burning like fire against hers.

'Um…I'd tell you that I…that I…'

His thumb began to stroke along the sensitive skin of her blue-veined wrist. 'How long?'

She ran her tongue over her lips, her stomach doing that little pony-kick thing again. 'I—I can't remember…'

He smiled a white-toothed smile. 'That makes two of us.'

She wrinkled her brow at him. 'You can't remember the last time you kissed a woman? What about your ex-wife?'

He gave her a rueful look. 'You know what they say about married couples.'

She stared, mesmerised by the movement of his lips as he spoke. He had such a beautiful mouth, the top lip sculpted and the bottom lip sensually full. There was no doubt in her mind that if that mouth took it upon itself to kiss hers, she was going to be in serious trouble. His thumb on her wrist was doing enough damage as it was; her belly was flip-flopping all over the place and her inner thighs already dampening with desire.

'Um… What do they say?' she managed to finally croak.

His gaze went to her mouth again. 'They say that once a couple is married, they forget how to kiss.'

She gave him a disbelieving glance. 'I'm sure that's not true.'

'Do you know any married couples who kiss like there's no tomorrow?'

Eloise couldn't help thinking of her foster-parents, who

hadn't even exchanged a quick peck on the cheek in the whole time she had been living with them. She had learned early on that they were uncomfortable with public shows of affection. Any attempts on her part had been met with stiff formality; she had felt at times as if she was leaning into a brick wall. They had held her at arm's length, as if frightened that too much affection would have her craving more than they could give.

'Er…no, but that doesn't mean they don't when they're in private,' she said. 'Kissing is a very intimate thing.'

'So you don't think we should do it right here where everyone can see us?' he asked ruefully.

'I'm not going to kiss you, Chief Inspector D'Ancey.' The sensible side of her knew it was a bad idea, but even so she could feel her heels lift off the back of her sodden sandals to bring her mouth within a breath of his.

'Not even once, just to see what happens?' he asked softly, his warm hint-of-mint breath skating lightly over the surface of her lips.

Eloise knew exactly what would happen. It would be fireworks and earthquakes and she knew she'd enjoy it. She couldn't afford to let it happen. It was madness to even think about the possibility.

But it was so tempting, so very tempting.

She could feel herself starting to cave in, the mingling of their breaths making it even harder for her to resist him.

It had been a very long time since she'd felt a man's arms around her—in fact, anyone's arms around her.

Standing in front of her was the most attractive man she had met in a very long time. And besides, she was a modern woman. Sex was a normal part of life in spite of what her foster-parents had preached.

But sex has consequences, a little voice inside her head

reminded her, especially for women. The emotional investment in a physical relationship was nearly always greater for
women. If she fell in love while over here on assignment,
where would that leave her?

She took an unsteady breath and forced her eyes away
from his mouth to meet his gaze. 'Not even once to see what
happens… Sorry…'

'Pity,' he said, releasing her hand and stepping back from
her. 'You know what they say about missed opportunities.'

Eloise rolled her eyes and hoped he couldn't see her lips
twitching in reluctant amusement. 'I'm not even going to ask.'

He grinned at her. 'Come on, you owe me a drink for pro-
viding you with emergency clothes. Did they fit, by the way?'

'I didn't try them on but, yes, I think they will, in spite of
what your daughter thinks of my figure.'

He gave her another amused glance. 'So that pressed a few
of your buttons, did it?'

'I know how to handle difficult teenagers.'

'Good, then maybe you can give me a few hints,' he said
with an element of wryness in his tone. 'Sometimes I can't
believe it's the same little girl I used to cradle in my arms
when she was a baby.'

Eloise found her eyes wandering to where his hands were
hanging by his sides, a vision of him holding a little baby
sending a warm river-like sensation through her belly. He had
nice hands, large and long fingered with a dusting of dark hair
running over the backs right up his arms.

'It must be hard learning when to let go,' she said into the
sudden silence.

'It is,' he said. 'The world is a dangerous place, especially
for young women. They think they're invincible but you and
I both know they are not.'

Eloise exchanged a grim look with him. 'I know.'

Another silence passed as they walked towards the Penhally Arms.

'You're not going to wear the clothes, are you?' he asked.

She gave him a sidelong glance as she passed him in the doorway. 'I'm not really a bright colour person. I guess that comes from too many years at a convent school where inward beauty was encouraged over outward.'

'You know what they say about hiding your talents under a bushel.'

Eloise couldn't stop her smile this time. 'You really like your sayings, don't you?'

His brown eyes twinkled as he pulled out a chair for her. 'Chief Inspector Cliché, that's me, or so my daughter thinks.'

Eloise waited until he was seated opposite before she said, 'Why don't you want me to talk to her?'

His eyes instantly lost their sparkle and a small frown criss-crossed his forehead. 'It is not your responsibility to interview the locals—that is my job and that of my colleagues. But in any case I would prefer her to be kept away from the investigation. It's got nothing to do with her. She barely knew the guy.'

'Not according to one of my sources,' she said, watching him closely.

He held her probing look but the line of his mouth tightened. 'You want to have a drink with me or play detectives?'

'I don't seem the harm in a bit of both.'

His top lip curled. 'I can see what you're doing, Dr Hayden. Your acceptance of a drink with me is all about pumping me for information, isn't it?'

'I'm sure you don't need me to remind you that if you're withholding information pertinent to the case, you could get into serious trouble,' she said. 'Poppy may be your daughter but if she's somehow involved in the suspicious death of Ethan Jenson, you'd better tell me now.'

'I told you she barely knew the guy.'

'I have reason to believe you're lying.'

His gaze hardened as it challenged hers. 'You think so?'

'You know what they say about gut feelings, Chief Inspector D'Ancey.'

'Hasn't anyone told you gut feelings don't stand up in court, Dr Hayden? If you want to solve this case then you'll need solid evidence and cold, hard facts.'

Eloise forced her chin up. 'I know that, you don't need to tell me how to do my job.'

'Tread carefully, Dr Hayden,' he warned in a low deep tone in case others nearby were listening. 'You might be after the biggest promotion of your career, but you're dealing with real people here and one of them happens to be my daughter. I won't allow you to use her as a stepladder to get where you want to go.'

'This isn't about my career,' she said, 'or your daughter for that matter. It's about a young man in the prime of his life who suddenly turned up dead. I want some answers for his family as well as the Australian government. That's what I'm being paid to do and forgive me if I've somehow got this wrong, but I was under the impression you were supposed to be helping me.'

Lachlan let a stiff silence pass before he sent one of his hands through his hair. 'Look,' he said on a tail end of a sigh, 'how about we drop the subject? Work takes up enough of my time and yours as it is. We're both off duty and can surely for the space of an hour or so talk about something else.'

Eloise felt one of his legs accidentally brush against hers. 'OK,' she said, tucking her legs well back. 'What shall we talk about?'

'Chief Inspector D'Ancey?' One of the barmaids rushed over with a worried expression on her face. 'There's some trouble with the some of the lads outside. Can you come and sort it out?'

Eloise suddenly became aware of the sound of jeering and swearing and glass breaking. Exchanging a brief glance with Lachlan, she followed him quickly outside.

CHAPTER FIVE

THE first thing Eloise noticed was the blood. There were great splotches of it on the cobblestones in the alley and even on one of the rubbish bins. She had to fight down her reaction. It had been several months since she'd attended the murder scene of a twenty-two-month-old girl and yet the sharp metallic scent of blood in the air brought it all back in an instant. Her skin felt clammy, her stomach churned and her head felt as if it had been placed in a vice.

'Quick! Cops!' A young male voice called out from further down the alley.

The gang of youths dispersed in all directions, one flying past Eloise so fast he very nearly knocked her from her already unsteady feet.

She watched as Lachlan caught another one in three fast strides, holding him up against the stone wall of the building. 'What's this about this time, Brian?' he asked. 'Do you want another assault charge on your record?'

The youth scowled at him. 'He started it,' he said, pointing to the young man who was now getting to his feet not far away from where Eloise was standing, blood pouring from a head wound.

Eloise went towards him. 'Are you all right?'

The young man wiped at his face, grimacing as he saw the blood. 'I'm fine,' he said. 'It was Davey I was worried about.'

She frowned and looked up and down the now deserted alleyway. 'Davey? Do you mean Davey Trevallyn?'

He nodded. 'The gang were hassling him. They do it all the time.'

'Where is he now?' she asked, handing him some tissues from her bag.

He mopped at his face, wincing slightly. 'I managed to get him out of the alley before the boys set on me.'

'I think you might need that wound looked at,' she said when she removed the tissues from his face. 'It might have some glass in it.'

'Yeah, I will. It feels like something's in there,' he said, wincing again as he dabbed at it. 'I'll see Dr Tremayne in the morning.'

'I think you should call him now,' Eloise said. 'Wounds like that can turn septic very quickly.'

'She's right, Robert,' Lachlan said, coming over to where they were standing. 'It looks nasty. Do you want to press charges?'

Robert shook his head. 'No, it won't do any good.'

'Brian's got it coming to him,' Lachlan said gravely. 'I let him go but I'll call on his parents tomorrow. He needs taking in hand.'

'It wasn't just him,' Robert said. 'You know what Gary Lovelace and his gang are like. They give Davey a hard time just for sport. It's sickening.'

'I know but it takes all types in this world,' Lachlan said. 'Come on, let's get you to the clinic and cleaned up. I'll give Dr Tremayne a call to meet us there.'

Eloise followed them out of the alley, listening as Lachlan

spoke to Nick Tremayne in his quiet but authoritative manner, his gaze flicking now and again to the young man by his side.

'You're the Australian police doctor, right?' Robert asked Eloise once they were on the Harbour Road. 'Poppy told me about you.'

Eloise smiled. 'You must be Robert Polgrean. Mrs Trevallyn told me you were Poppy's boyfriend.'

'"Was" being the operative word,' Robert said with an embittered look. 'We're not seeing each other any more.'

Eloise ignored the diamond-sharp look she was getting from Lachlan. 'Did you know Ethan Jenson at all?' she asked.

Robert's expression turned sour. 'He was a show pony if ever there was one,' he said. 'He changed girls more than he changed his board shorts.'

'Dr Hayden,' Lachlan interjected. 'Robert is bleeding, in pain and probably dazed from the roughing up he's had.'

'I do feel a bit faint…' Robert said, and before Eloise could reach him he crumpled to a heap on the pavement.

'Where's a doctor when you need one?' Lachlan said as he knelt down beside the boy and placed him in the recovery position.

'*I'm* a doctor,' Eloise said, feeling more than a little affronted.

'When was the last time you treated a live patient?' he asked.

'A fair while back,' she answered, 'but I haven't forgotten any of my resuscitation skills.'

'You might want to run those skills past him now,' he suggested. 'It's about four hundred metres to the clinic and I don't fancy carrying him.'

Eloise checked that Robert's airway was unobstructed and that his breathing was even. His pulse felt strong and about normal rate. 'Is it possible to call an ambulance?' she asked.

'No point,' he said, reaching for his mobile phone. 'They

would be half an hour coming from St Piran. I'll give Nick another call and get him to come this way.'

Within a few short minutes Robert had woken up and Nick arrived almost simultaneously. Robert was bundled into Nick's car and taken to the clinic, with Eloise and Lachlan riding in the back.

'I'm sorry about this,' Robert said as they entered the clinic. 'I don't know what came over me. I never faint.'

'It happens to the best of us,' Nick said, as he led the way into the clinic. 'I fainted at my first anatomy lesson. It was damned embarrassing.'

Eloise was expecting Nick put the young boy's mind at ease by chatting to him about inconsequential things while he cleansed the wound, as most doctors did, but instead he barely said a word. He injected some local anaesthetic and carefully removed a shard of glass embedded in the skin and inserted three stitches before he spoke again.

'I'll give you a short course of antibiotics to prevent infection. Your record here says you haven't had a tetanus booster for seven years, so I'll give you one now,' he said as he took off his gloves. 'I'll check the wound in a day or two, but in the meantime take it easy.'

'I will, Dr Tremayne, thank you. And thank you, Dr Hayden and Chief Inspector. You turned up at a good time,' Robert said.

'No problem, Robert,' Lachlan said patting him on the back. 'Do you want us to walk you home?'

'I'm going his way,' Nick said as he reached for his keys. 'You and Dr Hayden can get back to what you were doing.'

'We weren't doing anything,' Eloise said, and then blushed furiously as three male gazes turned to her. 'I mean…er… nothing important… Just work stuff…sort of…'

Nick gave a stiff on-off smile before turning back to his patient. 'Come on, Robert. Your mother will be wondering what's happened to you. How's your father, by the way? He hasn't been back to see me after his accident. Is he doing the exercises I gave him?'

'I think so,' Robert said, as he followed Nick outside.

Eloise glanced at Lachlan on their way out. 'This is all your fault, you know.'

'What's my fault?'

She pointed to Nick and his young patient a few steps ahead of them. 'It will be all over the village tomorrow and you know it,' she said in low whisper.

'What will be?'

She rolled her eyes at his innocent look. 'We were seen having a drink at the Penhally Arms.'

'I hate to contradict you, but we didn't actually get around to having a drink.'

Eloise had to look away from the temptation of his mouth. 'Yes, well, the service was a little slow,' she grumbled.

'We didn't have a drink because you were too busy trying to cross-examine me,' he said. 'The bar staff were probably too frightened to come over to take our order in case they were suddenly whipped up onto your makeshift witness stand.'

She gave him a droll look. 'The truth is, Chief Inspector, *you* were too busy trying to withhold information from me.'

'Actually, I was too busy thinking about how it would feel to kiss you.'

Eloise stared at him for a moment, her mouth opening and closing like that of a fish. 'I'm going to pretend you didn't say that.'

'It's true, Eloise,' he said. 'Or do you prefer being called Ellie?'

She turned away. 'No, I don't.'

'You have something against shortened names?'

'I have something against men who won't accept no for an answer,' she said. 'I'm here to work. I'm not interested in taking the place of your ex-wife.'

'I wasn't exactly offering you marriage.'

She turned around to look at him. 'Just what is it you are offering, Chief Inspector D'Ancey? A quick fling to pass the time until someone more suitable comes along?'

His rueful smile totally disarmed her. 'I'm not very good at this, am I? Too long out of the saddle, isn't that would you would say back in Australia?'

She pursed her mouth at him. 'I'm sure it's like riding a bike, you never forget the steps.'

'Have you had dinner?' he asked.

Here we go again, Eloise thought. Did this man not understand the word 'no'? 'You're asking me to have dinner with you?' she asked.

'Just dinner,' he said, with another one of his stomach-tilting smiles. 'I wouldn't rule out a kiss, though, but maybe just one to be on the safe side.'

'What about your daughter?' she asked, trying her best to ignore the way her heart was jumping about in her chest at the thought of feeling that mouth pressed against hers. 'Shouldn't you be at home, looking after her?'

'Poppy is staying with her friend tonight,' he said. 'I'm a free man.'

She gave him a probing look. 'Have you checked that she is actually where she says she is?'

A small frown creased his brow. 'Listen, Dr Hayden, my daughter isn't out all the time neither does she sleep around if that's what you're thinking. I admit she's young and wilful but, then, she hasn't long witnessed her parents going through a difficult divorce. I also admit she's no angel, but if she says she's staying at her friend's house, I see no need to check up on her. It's tantamount to a betrayal of trust.'

'It's also your duty as a parent,' she pointed out. 'Do you know how many parents I have met who thought their kids were safe at a friend's house, only to have to go and identify them at the morgue the following day?'

His jaw tightened. 'You've been in forensics too long, Dr Hayden. You're seeing everyone as a potential victim.'

'I thought you said I didn't have enough experience?' she said with a little jut of her chin.

'The experience you've had has obviously coloured your judgement,' he said. 'Is that why you put your hand up for this job—to get away from something too distressing for you to get to sleep at night?'

Eloise blinked at him, her mouth going dry as little Jessica Richardson's features swam before her eyes. The last autopsy she'd done before she'd left, she would vividly remember that tiny body, still dressed in a pink fairy costume, her skin porcelain pale in death.

'Are you all right?' Lachlan asked, touching her on the arm.

She bit her bottom lip, struggling for control. 'Jet-lag,' she said, blowing out a ragged breath. 'I guess I haven't adjusted yet.'

His hand was warm and solid on the bare skin of her forearm. She looked down at it, her whole body registering the tingle of his flesh where it connected with hers. What would it feel like to have his mouth and tongue rub and stroke against hers? What would it feel like to have his hands shape her breasts, or slide down her thighs, or even delve into that secret place between them that had been empty for so long?

'You need some food,' he said. 'If you're not comfortable

with eating in public with me then why not come back to my house and have something with me there? It's not far from here, if you think your foot will manage it.'

Eloise could feel herself weakening. She didn't feel like spending her first night in Cornwall on her own. She had spent far too many nights alone with pink fairy wings flapping inside her head to torment her. 'I can get something back at the guest-house...' she said.

'Yes, like food poisoning,' he said with one of his sudden and totally disarming grins. 'Bea Trevallyn isn't the best cook in the world and certainly not the most hygienic. The place was almost closed down a few months back after a salmonella outbreak.'

Eloise gave a whole-body shiver. 'You're seriously starting to tempt me,' she confessed.

'Good,' he said. 'I'm not quite up to celebrity chef standard or anything but I can rustle up something to get by.'

'Are you sure you don't mind?' she asked, reluctantly removing her arm from the comforting hold of his.

His smile this time revealed his two crossed bottom teeth. 'You know what they say about rejecting an invitation the first time around.'

'OK, what *do* they say?' Eloise asked, as she fell into step beside him, a small smile beginning to tug at her mouth.

He glinted down at her. 'You might not get another chance. The invitation might not be repeated and you could have missed a golden opportunity that you might end up regretting for the rest of your life.'

'I make a point of not dwelling on regrets,' she said as she looked away. 'They don't change anything.'

Lachlan glanced at her bent head, taking in her pleated brow and the downturn of her mouth. Dr Eloise Hayden may be a career-woman on a mission but she had a soft side that she valiantly tried to keep hidden. He couldn't help wondering what she had faced so far in her career to make her present such a tough, suffer-no-fools-gladly exterior. He knew it was a tough call, being a forensics specialist. He had seen many a colleague turn to alcohol to try and block out the images of gruesome murder scenes or heavily decomposed bodies. Their relationships suffered as well. It was hard to deal with distressed relatives of victims while trying to maintain their own family relationships. Divorce rates were high in the force and higher still amongst top-level officers. He often wondered if his career had had more to do with his divorce from Margaret than anything else. She hadn't really understood the demands of the job and had come to resent the unpredictable hours he had worked. He had learned the hard way to loosen up a bit. He didn't want to do what so many did and burn out completely.

'What do you think of Nick Tremayne?' he asked as they walked up a slight incline to his house.

'He's seems very competent,' Eloise answered. 'But I have a feeling he's not comfortable dealing with me. I spoke to Kate Althorp earlier and she said he's like that with everybody.' She sent him a quick glance. 'Is there something going on between them?'

Lachlan gave a could-mean-anything shrug. 'Hard to tell,' he said. 'Nick is a bit of a closed book. He lost his wife Annabel to peritonitis a couple of years back. He blamed the surgeon at St Piran Hospital for her death. Nick's a hard nut to crack—pretty much keeps to himself, if you know what I mean. I guess it's understandable really. He still feels he would have been able to save Annabel if he'd got there in time, but Ben Carter did his best. Ben's his son-in-law now so things have settled down in that quarter. Nick of all people should know it happens like that sometimes. Cases go horribly wrong and no one's really to blame. The human body is not something you can predict the outcomes of in regard to medical intervention. Patients and relatives still expect things will turn out perfectly every time.'

Eloise glanced up at him again. 'You sound like you really understand the life of a medico.'

He gave her a brief smile before looking away. 'My father was a doctor, an O and G specialist, actually.'

'Was?'

His smile faded a little as he stopped outside a white house, his hand going to the back pocket of his jeans for the keys. 'He died a few years back,' he said. 'A ruptured aneurysm. My mother has never really come to terms with it. A bit like Nick, she feels guilty that she didn't see the signs in time.'

'Doctors make the very worst patients,' she said as she followed him into the cottage. 'They think they're bullet-proof. I guess it comes from years of diagnosing everyone else's ailments. You think it will never happen to you.'

'What about your background?' he asked, as he closed the door of the cottage. 'What do your parents do?'

'I don't have parents,' she said and looked away from his penetrating gaze. 'Or at least not real ones,' she added with a rueful twist to her mouth. 'I was brought up by foster-parents.'

'Tough call.'

She turned to face him, the empathetic warmth of his expression making her chest feel as if something similar to rapidly rising bread dough had been placed in it. 'Yes,' she said. 'It was.'

'And still is?'

Eloise had to look away from that all-seeing gaze. 'I'm over it,' she said. 'My foster-parents have been good, better than good actually. They have made it their life's work to ensure I was kept on the straight and narrow.'

'And have they succeeded?' he asked, as he reached for a bottle of red wine and two glasses.

She couldn't help a small wry smile as she took the glass of wine he poured for her, meeting his dark eyes in the process. 'They would be shocked to see me right now,' she said, indicating the glass in her hand. 'They're staunch teetotallers.'

He smiled one of his spine-loosening smiles as he raised his glass to hers in a toast. 'To the moral corruption of Dr Eloise Hayden from Australia,' he said.

She twisted her mouth at him. 'I'm not sure I should drink to that.'

He smiled at her over the top of his glass. 'You have some other suggestion?'

She touched her glass against his, the sound of it a little loud in the silence. 'To finding out the truth about Ethan Jenson's death,' she said.

He brought his glass to his lips, his eyes still holding hers.

Eloise felt the irresistible pull of his gaze and took another sip of wine to distract herself. She was a little stunned by her reaction to him. It was not her style at all to become infatuated with someone so quickly. She wondered if it was her hormones or something. He was undoubtedly one of the most attractive men she had encountered in a very long time but that didn't mean she had to fall into bed with him. Her foster-parents would be appalled to think she was considering having an affair with a divorced man. According to their beliefs, such a union was taboo and the fact he had a teenage daughter would make it a million times worse.

Not that she was considering having an affair with him or anyone, she quickly reassured herself. She was here to work, that's all. After all, a month was hardly long enough to get to know someone enough to make such a commitment.

She took another sip of wine, enjoying the black cherry and hint of cinnamon taste on her tongue, wondering if she should say something to break the little silence, but before she could think of something work related and safe, Lachlan swooped in under her defences and asked, 'So what happened to your real parents?'

CHAPTER SIX

ELOISE did her best to disguise the slight tremble of her hand as she lowered her glass to the kitchen counter. 'They died a long time ago.'

'How old were you?'

She tucked a strand of her hair behind one ear and lowered her eyes from the probe of his. 'I was eight…almost nine.'

'An accident?'

She met his eyes briefly. 'I'm not sure about my father,' she said, looking away again. 'I've never met him. I don't think my mother even knew who he was, actually.' She paused for a moment before adding, 'She died of a drug overdose.'

'That must have been a hard thing to deal with as a small child,' he said. 'Were there no other relatives to take you in?'

She gave him an embittered movement of her lips. 'Yes. I had grandparents but they hadn't spoken to my mother for years. They weren't interested in taking in her child. They considered me the spawn of the devil and wanted absolutely nothing to do with me.'

Lachlan frowned. 'You were an innocent child, for God's sake. How could they blame you for your mother's actions?'

'My mother dabbled with drugs during her teens and had me just after she turned eighteen. I think I was the result of a one-night stand with a dealer,' Eloise said in a tone stripped of emotion. 'She was a heroin addict by the age of twenty-one, Chief Inspector. I'm sure you've met plenty like her in your line of work, just as I have done. She slept with anyone she could to feed her habit. She died at the age of twenty-seven. She was three times my age at the time of her death but I always felt as if I was the adult.'

'How did you survive such an upbringing?' he asked.

She gave a little shrug. 'How does anyone survive?' she asked. 'You and I have both dealt with the other victims of crime—the relatives of the perpetrator. They live with the shame of what their loved ones have done. They become outcasts, untouchables if you like. My maternal grandparents considered me beyond redemption, having been exposed to such depravity for so long. They assumed I would turn out just like their daughter so to spare themselves further heartbreak they cut all ties with me.'

'Is that why you're on the other side of the law?' he asked. 'To prove a point to them so to speak?'

She let out a tiny sigh. 'I guess to some degree—yes. I wanted to show that no matter what background you come from you can rise above it if you have enough determination. I loved my mother but she had a problem that was too big to fix and I was far too young to help her. Knowing what I know now about addiction, and if I'd been even a little bit older, I could have got her into some sort of programme. It might have helped. I know it doesn't always but I like to think it would have in her case. I think she really wanted to get straight. She hated her life. She hated putting me through it but she was caught in a cycle of addiction that was too strong for her.'

In the small pause that ensued Eloise felt the warm pressure of his brown eyes on her. He didn't offer any useless platitudes but listened in a respectful silence that somehow gave her the courage to reveal more than she had ever done before—to anyone.

'My grandparents didn't want anything to do with her,' she carried on after another beat or two of silence. 'They were both well-to-do academics with high-profile lecturing positions at a Sydney university. They just couldn't cope with the shame of having their once academically brilliant daughter dropping out of her studies to have a child out of wedlock, let alone to go on to sell herself to get her next high. She stole from them and some of their friends so many times they eventually placed a restraining order on her.'

'I admire you for what you've achieved,' he said, his voice deep and gravelly. 'It must have taken a lot of guts to get where you've got.'

'My foster-parents were determined to do their bit to salvage me,' she said. 'They took me on as a sort of project, I think. I resented them for years, out of loneliness and frustration, I expect, but deep down I think they wanted the best for me, even if they didn't always feel entirely comfortable about my background.'

'Are you close to them?'

She gave another little shrug. 'No… I don't think anyone can ever take the place of your mother. My mother would never have made the first-round criteria of mother of the year or anything, but she loved me. I never doubted it. The trouble was, heroin got there first. It was her first priority and was until the day she died.'

'And here I am worrying about Poppy,' he said wryly. 'I need to get a grip or, as she says, take a chill pill.'

Eloise met his warm gaze. 'You have every right to worry about her,' she said. 'She's your daughter and you love her. She needs protecting. She's at that terribly vulnerable age—not quite an adult, not really a child. It must be hard, doing it alone.'

He gave her a twisted smile. 'To tell you the truth, I've often felt as if I've always been doing it on my own,' he said. 'Margaret never really wanted a child. We got caught out while we were dating. Contraception isn't always foolproof and certainly back then even less so. We were faced with the agonising decision of terminating or carrying on. I was twenty-three years old, she was twenty-two. We didn't have two pennies to rub together but somehow I managed to convince her to keep the baby.'

Eloise was surprised it had been him to do so. So often it was the man in the relationship who wanted the easy way out. It made her realise there was more to Lachlan D'Ancey than she had given him credit for.

'We got married later that summer,' he went on. 'It wasn't a happy marriage from the word go. Margaret had had her career path all mapped out and never let me forget it was my fault it had been thwarted. It was a difficult pregnancy and Poppy was an unsettled baby. We lived a long way from any relatives who might have helped out a bit. And of course my shift work didn't help. I never seemed to be there when she needed it most.'

'I'm sorry,' Eloise said. 'It must have been very hard for both of you. Are you on better terms now that you're divorced?'

He leaned back against the counter, cradling his glass in one hand. 'The bond of a child is not something you can sign away on the piece of paper that dissolves a marriage. Margaret sacrificed a lot in agreeing to go through with the pregnancy. She could have just as easily ignored my wishes and got on with her life, but she didn't and I will always admire her for that. But as for being friends…' He let out a breath that sounded as if it had come from deep within him. 'We're friends but not particularly close. Besides, it wouldn't be appropriate now that she has Roger as her partner.'

'How does Poppy get on with her mother's boyfriend?'

'She doesn't say much,' he answered. 'I think she worries it might upset me or something.' His mouth lifted in a smile as he added, 'I know she was a bit rude towards you this afternoon but I think she's really pretty keen on finding me a replacement.'

Eloise could feel her cheeks warming as he held her gaze. 'Why is that?' she asked. 'Most girls her age would prefer not to have to compete for their father's attention with another woman. I hear horror stories all the time over blended families and the rivalry that goes on. It can get pretty ugly, or so I'm told.'

'I know, I've seen it myself and, as you say, it can be *very* ugly.' He let out a little sigh and added, 'I've often thought Poppy might have been happier if she'd had a brother or sister, especially now that Margaret and I aren't together any more. She begged her mother for years to have another child but Margaret wouldn't hear of it.'

'What about you?' she asked, surprised yet again at her audacity at asking him such a personal question. 'Would you have liked another child?'

Lachlan gave the contents of his glass a little swirl, watching as the wine left a light film higher on the bowl of the glass. 'I grew up with two siblings, a younger brother and sister. We had a great time, playing in the back garden, building tree-houses, playing cricket or swimming in the stream at the back of the village green. I would have liked Poppy to have had a similar childhood, but it wasn't to be.'

'It's not too late,' she said. 'You could easily have another child or two.'

His eyes came back to hers, a mischievous twinkle lurking in the brown depths. 'Are you auditioning for the job, Dr Hayden?'

Eloise felt her cheeks flame all over again and to disguise her discomfiture said in a dismissive tone, 'And give up my career? I don't think so. I've worked too hard and for too long to stand in some man's kitchen barefoot and pregnant.'

'You know what they say about women who put their careers ahead of having a husband and family,' he said.

'Yes, I do, actually,' she answered curtly. 'They have freedom and lots of money and luxurious holidays without tears and tantrums.'

'They also end up lonely in their old age.'

'That's funny because I know plenty of married women with children who are desperately lonely,' she argued. 'They've spent their lives giving everything to their families, only to have them leave without a backward glance. Then to add insult to injury their husbands exchange them for a newer version. It totally stinks.'

'So you're not prepared to risk it?' he asked.

She let out a little almost inaudible sigh. 'I thought about it once…but it ended in tears.'

'Yours or his?'

Her eyes came back to his. 'I'd been warned before that dating a colleague was asking for trouble,' she said. 'I foolishly thought I could get away with it but it backfired horribly. As soon as word got out in our department that we were seeing each other, life became unbearable for both of us. I bailed out first.'

'How did he take it?'

She gave him a jaded look. 'He married a hairdresser three months later.'

He winced. 'That must have hurt.'

'Not as much as it probably should have,' she said. 'I guess if I'd really been in love with him I would have been devastated, but I wasn't. I went back to work the next day and sat down at the desk three away from his and carried on.'

'Have you ever been in love?' he asked, as he reached to top up her glass. 'As in weak-at-the-knees-heart thumping-can't-think-of-anything-else type of love?'

Eloise felt her whole body react as his hand briefly brushed against hers as he held her glass steady. She avoided his gaze, trying to get her heart rate to return to somewhere near normal, her stomach leaping and diving as she breathed in his male scent. That alluring hint of musk and citrus, the warmth of his body, the sheer bulk of it so close to hers, the impulse to reach out and touch the peppery shadow of evening growth on his lean jaw almost more than she could bear.

It must be the wine, she thought, eyeing it suspiciously as he poured it into her glass. Red wine was lethal when it came to self-control. It made people do things they wouldn't normally do. The relaxation of inhibitions, she saw it all the time in her line of work. Perfectly rational intelligent people did outrageous things under the influence of alcohol. She was clearly no different and would have to watch herself in future, especially around someone as seriously tempting as Lachlan D'Ancey.

'No,' she finally managed to croak out as she raised her glass to her lips. 'What about you?'

He held her gaze for several pulsating seconds. 'No,' he said. 'I'm a bit ashamed to say I didn't love Margaret in that way. I cared about her, I still do and very deeply, but I never felt like I couldn't live without her or anything. As I said, we got caught out and in another time and place we would never have ended up together.'

'But you have Poppy.'

He smiled a smile that totally transformed his features. 'Yes, I have Poppy.'

'And you would do anything to protect her, wouldn't you?'

Lachlan's brows came together in a wary frown. 'What exactly are you saying, Dr Hayden?'

'I'm saying that I am here to investigate a suspicious death,' she said. 'A death of a person it is alleged your daughter had an intimate relationship with in the days before he died.'

He put down his glass with a sharp little crack. 'That is hearsay, not a substantiated fact.'

'Not according to Robert Polgrean.'

'Robert is an eighteen-year-old boy who has fancied himself in love with my daughter for years,' he bit out.

'Davey Trevallyn saw Ethan Jenson and your daughter on the beach together,' she said. 'Beatrice told me.'

He threw his hands in the air in disgust. 'Beatrice Trevallyn believes everything her son tells her, but it doesn't mean a word of it is true. He's has learning difficulties, Dr Hayden. Please don't misunderstand me, I'm not discounting him as a person or even as a reliable witness, but you have to factor in that he is operating mentally at the age of about ten.'

'So you don't believe your daughter was seeing Ethan Jenson?'

He set his jaw. 'She told you herself, she met him once or twice.'

'So you don't think she was sleeping with him?'

He frowned at her darkly. 'What sort of question is that?' he asked. 'Of course she wasn't sleeping with him.'

'Had she been sleeping with Robert Polgrean?'

You're taking way too long to answer, Lachlan thought as Eloise's gaze penetrated his.

He hated to think of his little girl becoming intimate with anyone. Robert was about the only person he could envisage as a potential son-in-law but not until years had passed. But most fathers would feel the same about their daughters, he realised. Poppy was sixteen. Sure, she looked and acted a whole lot older but she was still—in his eyes at least—a little girl.

His little girl.

'No,' he said firmly.

Eloise gave a little snort of derision. 'Do you realise most teenage girls these days have had sex by the age of fourteen?'

'I know the statistics, Dr Hayden, but I also know my daughter,' he said. 'She's not the sleep-around type.'

'That's what every parent says. No one wants to think of their son or daughter being sexually active too early but hormones make it virtually impossible for most young people to resist temptation.'

'What about you, Dr Hayden?' he asked with a mocking smile. 'How are you at resisting temptation?'

Eloise tightened her mouth. 'We're not talking about me, Chief Inspector D'Ancey,' she clipped out. 'We're talking about your daughter. You say she's at a friend's house this evening, but what if she isn't? What if she lied to you so she could meet someone in secret, someone you might not approve of, such as Ethan Jenson?'

'Ethan Jenson is dead.'

Her chin came up. 'I know, but he wasn't a little over a week ago, was he?'

His brown gaze burned like a furnace, his expression nothing short of incredulous. 'Are you suggesting *I* had something to do with Ethan Jenson's death?'

'Kate Althorp told me there were a lot of fathers of teenage girls in the district who would be very glad he was out of the way. You could easily be one of them, irrespective of your standing in the community.'

'Those are very serious accusations,' he said. 'If I were you, I would be very careful who I voiced them to, otherwise you could find yourself in very deep water.'

Her eyes glinted challengingly as she held his heated gaze. 'Interesting choice of words, Chief Inspector, don't you think?'

His mouth flattened into a thin white line. A little flutter of alarm disturbed the lining of Eloise's stomach as he stepped towards her. She made to move backwards but came up against the pantry door, the small round knob of the handle digging into the middle of her back.

Then his eyes locked down on hers, glittering with sparks of anger, but there was something else that was far more dangerous.

Male desire...

CHAPTER SEVEN

'W-WHAT are you doing?' Eloise croaked as his body loomed closer.

'What do you think I'm doing?' he asked.

She swallowed and her wobbly belly did another little tumble turn as his chest almost but not quite brushed against hers. 'Stop it immediately.'

He raised his hands in the air. 'I'm not even touching you.'

She ran her tongue over the dryness of her lips. 'I can feel your body heat… That's…that's touching in my book.'

'I haven't read that particular book,' he said, his warm breath caressing her face as his hands came to rest either side of her head on the pantry door. 'Is it worth reading?'

Eloise was having trouble keeping focused on what he was saying. In fact, she was having trouble stringing two thoughts together in her head. All she could focus on was his mouth—his beautifully shaped mouth with its fuller bottom lip that she knew would be nothing short of sensual heaven pressing against hers. This close she could see each masculine pinpoint of dark stubble over his top lip, and the skin of her face began to tingle in anticipation of feeling its abrasiveness against the softness of her face. Her breasts felt tight and tender at the same time, their nipples suddenly aching for the press of his hands, the exploration of his fingers, the heat and fire of his tongue, and the primitive and enthralling scrape of his teeth.

She felt like her body was on fire. Flames were leaping between her legs, sending spot fires to every part of her body. Her brain was zinging with images of their bodies locked together in passion, his hard maleness buried in her feminine softness, the rocking motion of their sexual union making her femininity weep with desire to feel it for real instead of just imagining it.

She arched her back away from the pantry doorknob and her whole body jolted with sensual shock as her body came into full contact with his, from chest to pelvis.

His eyes fastened on hers.

Her heart came to a shuddering halt before kick-starting again with a series of out-of-beat heavy thuds.

Her mouth went dry.

His mouth was close, so close she could feel his breath moving over the achingly sensitive surface of her lips like an invisible feather being brushed along them.

'*You're* touching me,' he said, his voice sounding as if it had been scraped over a rough surface.

'It's the doorknob…' She hitched in a jagged breath. 'It was digging a hole in my back.'

He smiled crookedly. 'And here I was thinking you were coming onto me.'

'I wasn't coming onto you,' she said, knowing it was nothing but a bare-faced lie. She had never wanted a man to kiss her more in her entire life. Her lips burned with the need to feel the hard searching pressure of his. Surely he could see it? How could she hide her longing? It thrummed in her veins like a fast-flowing river of need, the pulse of it so strong it threatened to break through the tender barrier of her skin.

His eyes went to her mouth. 'Are you sure?'

She moistened her lips again. 'P-pretty sure…'

His smile widened. 'So you're in two minds about taking this one step further, are you, Dr Hayden from Australia?'

Eloise swallowed again, her throat feeling far too narrow and dry. 'You know what they say about mixing business and pleasure, Chief Inspector D'Ancey,' she said in a breathless whisper.

'What do they say?' he asked, bringing his mouth to just above hers.

'It's…it's dangerous…'

He cocked one brow. 'Dangerous? How so?'

'It makes things hazy…you know…it colours your judgement until you can't think straight. It's not very…er… professional…'

He very slowly reached to brush a wayward strand of her hair back from her mouth, and gently tucked it behind her ear. 'So you don't think we should continue with this?' he asked.

She compressed her lips just once to see if the tingling sensation would go away, but if anything it made it even worse. 'Um…' *Oh, God, why did he have to have such a kissable mouth?* she thought. It was so strong and yet so soft and so very close to hers.

Way too close.

And his hands were so long fingered and masculine and yet gentle at the same time. She could almost imagine them skating over her naked skin, touching her, shaping her until she was a mindless pool of need.

'Are you usually so indecisive, Dr Hayden?' he asked with another bone-melting smile.

'I'm not sure…'

He laughed and stepped back from her. 'I promised you

dinner. I'd better get on with it. What do you fancy? I have some fresh fish Timmy Ennor dropped in earlier or I can rustle up an omelette.'

Eloise blinked once or twice to reorient herself. *He was talking about food at a time like this?* Wasn't he the least bit affected by that little interlude? Her heart was still doing star-jumps in her chest while he was preparing to toss a salad.

Men!

Who could make them out? They must have some sort of on-off switch when it came to desire. Hers was still silently smouldering, threatening to blow the circuit board of her body every time he looked her way.

'Um…whatever is fine…' she mumbled.

She watched as he began assembling ingredients on the kitchen counter, her heart rate still struggling to find its normal rhythm.

She had never met anyone like Lachlan D'Ancey before. He made her feel like an incompetent junior colleague one minute and a melting female wanton the next. She wondered if he was leading her on deliberately, toying with her to see how far he could go. She knew plenty of men who were like that. They saw female colleagues as easy targets, someone to pass the time with, a supposedly harmless affair to break the boredom of routine investigations. It wouldn't be the first time two colleagues thrown together on a case ended up intimately involved with each other. Emotions ran high during certain investigations. Life-and-death situations often triggered the most primal of all responses which later on, when things cooled down, were nearly always seriously regretted. She knew of at least three marriages that had broken up as a result of such affairs that on a different day might not have occurred.

Her life was complicated enough as it was. She had plans

for her future that held little room for intimate attachments. And even though a secret part deep inside of her longed for the security of a loving long-term relationship, the thought of bringing a child or two into the world that held so many dangers terrified her. What if she had a little Jessica, for instance?

A vision of Jessica's mother's grief-stricken face swam before her eyes.

Lachlan turned around from the refrigerator to see Eloise looking vacantly into space, her expression haunted with shadows he could see reflected in her china-blue eyes.

'So why did you take on this particular case?' he asked, handing her the glass of wine she'd abandoned earlier. 'It wasn't just about the prospects of a promotion, was it?'

She appeared to give herself a mental shake as she took the wine from him. She looked into the contents of the glass for a moment before answering in a soft tone. 'No, not really, although I do want to move up the career ladder. I had a tough case I had to deal with some months ago. I haven't found it easy to move on.'

'Do you want to talk about it?'

She gave him a rueful smile. 'If I thought talking would bring back to life a not quite two-year-old girl and hand her back to her totally devastated mother then, yes, I'd talk until the cows came home, but it won't, will it?'

Lachlan placed a bowl of salad to the table. 'I had to head the investigation of a case of two missing twelve-year-old boys a few years back. It was the biggest search with over four hundred officers involved. It went on for over a month and covered several counties.'

'Did you find them?'

He gave her a grim look. 'A junior officer eventually found them inside a concrete bridge pylon. They had obviously fallen in the day they were reported missing. No one heard their cries for help.'

'Oh, God…'

He blew out a ragged sigh. 'The forensics team had a hard time of it. The younger one working on the case later committed suicide. He couldn't handle the images in his head from being at the scene.'

Eloise gulped back a swallow. 'How do you handle it? The images of what you have to see and do?'

He pulled out a chair for her to sit down. 'I do what most other police officers do. We have a drink and a debriefing chat that at some point usually involves some sort of black humour before returning home to our homes and pretending everything's normal.'

'But it isn't, is it?' she asked softly. 'It can never be normal.'

'No, but if we allow it to invade our every waking moment, we'd all end up like that young forensics guy. We have a job to do and, yes, it's not always pretty or even very rewarding at times, but it has to be done.'

Eloise sat on the chair and laid her serviette across her lap. 'Did you ever consider any other career?' she asked.

He smiled as he placed a salad on the table. 'I think for a time my parents hoped I'd follow in my father's footsteps but I was never really interested in becoming a doctor.'

'Why was that?'

'I had a slight run-in with a cop when I was fifteen,' he said. 'It was nothing serious—it was just a bit of a lark on my part. He could have hauled me over the coals for it but instead he sat me down at the station and talked to me about choices, how the choices we make in our youth seal our fate in adulthood. It really made an impression on me. If he'd ranted and raved and threatened jail, it wouldn't have been half as effective.'

'Is that why you have a reputation for being fairly easy-going?' she asked. 'Kate Althorp said you were greatly admired in the community.'

'I uphold the law but I don't hit people over the head with it unless it's warranted,' he said. 'Brian, for instance, the kid who was in the alley with Robert? He's not a bad kid. He's got a rough sort of background. His father's a drunk who comes and goes when he feels like it and his mother struggles periodically with depression. Brian doesn't need detention, he needs attention, he's crying out for it. That's why he hangs around with Gary Lovelace's gang of youths. He longs to belong some-where to someone, even if they're less than desirable.'

Eloise couldn't help feeling impressed with his take on things. So many of her male colleagues relished in brandish-ing the power their position afforded them. Lachlan, however, seemed to really understand the issues in young people's lives, perhaps because he was the father of a teenager himself.

'What about you?' he asked. 'Do you have a sure-fire way of dealing with things?'

She toyed with her wineglass as she thought about it. 'I exercise a bit, walking mostly. I've never been much of a gym bunny, I'm afraid. I like to be alone to process things.'

'Sounds good to me. I do the same. There are some great walks through the farming districts. The roads are narrow but there's not much traffic.'

She gave him another wry smile. 'I don't suppose your daughter has a pair of walking shoes in my size she could lend me till my luggage arrives?'

He smiled back. 'My daughter's idea of sport is lying on the beach, looking at the surfers. I'm not even sure if she owns a pair of trainers. If she does, I can assure you they've never been used.'

'She's very beautiful.'

'She takes after her mother.'

A pang of something that felt like jealousy suddenly stabbed at Eloise's insides. She knew she wasn't exactly in danger of stopping any clocks or anything but neither did she consider herself model material. Her figure was trim and her features classical enough to be considered attractive, but she never felt comfortable without a bit of make-up on. She wasn't sure why she felt that way. Her foster-mother thought it was vain and frowned in disapproval at the very hint of lip-gloss but Eloise had stuck to her guns and used both make-up and perfume to remind herself she was still a woman, even if she was working in what was still considered predominately a man's world.

'Would you like more wine?' Lachlan asked, holding up the bottle.

Eloise twisted her mouth. 'You know what they say about wine, Chief Inspector D'Ancey.'

He grinned at her. 'I do, actually. Erasmus said it. "*In vino veritas*" —in wine there is truth.'

She smiled. 'I'm impressed. I didn't know you were a Latin scholar.'

'I studied it at school,' he said. 'You mentioned you went to a convent school. What was that like?'

'It was strict but the nuns were generally very nice. I had a favourite, Sister Patricia. She was younger than the others and, while not exactly progressive, she always made me feel as if I was special in some way.'

'I am sure you were and still are special.'

Eloise felt her cheeks grow warm. 'She also warned me about men like you,' she said, looking at him from beneath her lashes.

He lifted his eyebrows in a guileless manner. '*Moi?*'

'You're a natural flirt, Chief Inspector D'Ancey and I'm not going to fall for it,' she said primly.

'You think I'm flirting with you?'

She tried her best to frown at him. 'Aren't you?'

He smiled that boyish smile again. 'I'm probably horribly out of practice but, yes, I am and I'm enjoying it immensely. You blush like a schoolgirl every time I look at you.'

She looked down at her plate rather than meet his eyes. 'I'm a bit out of practice, too,' she admitted. 'I really don't mean to give you the wrong impression. I told you before, I'm not here to have a quick fling.'

'If you change your mind, put me at the top of the list of potential candidates.'

She rolled her eyes at him. 'You really need to work on your pick-up lines,' she said. 'That was totally pathetic.'

'Was it?' He chuckled as he handed her the salad dressing. 'I thought that was going to have you fall for me before dessert for sure.'

'Dessert?' Her blue eyes began to sparkle. 'Now, that *is* a pick-up line. What did you have in mind?'

'I'm not sure if I should tell you,' he said. 'You might think I was coming onto to you.'

'Aren't you?'

'What do you think?'

That was the whole trouble, Eloise thought. She didn't know what to think. Her normally rational-do-it-by-the-book mind had been scrambled ever since she'd set eyes on Chief Inspector Lachlan D'Ancey. He rattled her in every way possible. She had never experienced anything like it before in her life. Her brief encounter with Bill had been nothing compared to this. Bill had not moved her quite the way Lachlan's smiles had done.

And even though she kept telling herself Lachlan was divorced with a teenage daughter who, according to Eloise's gut feeling, was somehow involved in the case she was supposed to be investigating, all that seemed to be secondary to what was going on between them now.

She felt it like a pulse in the room. The air was thick and heavy with it.

Attraction.

Male and female.

Uncontrollable.

Forbidden and dangerous.

Irresistible.

'I have some raspberries from Rona Troon's farm,' he said breaking the tension. 'And some wickedly sinful clotted cream from the Hendry dairy farm. Are you tempted?'

'I'm seriously tempted,' Eloise said, but somehow she felt sure that Chief Inspector D'Ancey knew she wasn't talking about raspberries and cream.

CHAPTER EIGHT

'WOULD YOU LIKE a coffee, Dr Hayden?' Lachlan asked as he began to clear their dessert plates from the table.

'No, thank you, and, please, call me Eloise,' she said.

'But not Ellie, right?'

She frowned and rose to help him with clearing the table. 'No…'

'Is that what your mother called you?'

Her hand froze on the glass she had reached to lift from the table. She took a steadying breath and lifted her eyes back to his. 'I just prefer Eloise.'

'Too many bad memories?'

'Now who's playing detective?' she asked with a sharp edge to her tone.

His eyes met hers in a challenge. 'You're a closed book, Eloise Hayden, and I don't like closed books.'

'Tough,' she said with a toss of her head. 'I'm not here to tell you my life story. I'm here to investigate Ethan Jenson's death.' She reached for her purse and key to Trevallyn House. 'Thank you for dinner. I think it's probably time for me to get back to the guest-house.'

'I'll walk you back and don't waste your breath arguing with me.'

'I don't need an escort,' she threw back. 'It's barely four blocks from here.'

'It might only be four streets away but you are a single woman in a village you don't know.'

'I'm trained in self-defence.'

His mouth tilted mockingly. 'You're what? Five foot six and weigh about a hundred and ten pounds, if that. You wouldn't have a hope of fending off an attacker bigger than you.'

She pulled her shoulders back, her eyes glinting with determination. 'All right,' she said. 'I'll prove it. Try and get me in a head lock.'

He looked at her incredulously. 'You're surely not serious?'

She lifted her chin. 'Go on, Chief Inspector. Give it to me. I'll show you how I can—*Oomph!*'

Eloise realised later she'd really had no hope of getting out of *that* particular hold. She didn't even think of trying. As soon as Lachlan's mouth came down and captured hers, every single self-defence manoeuvre was wiped from her brain like a virus did to a computer hard drive.

His lips moved over the surface of hers with almost lazy intent, as if he had all the time in the world and he knew no one—least of all her—was going to stop him. His tongue stroked for entry, just the once, and her lips opened on a sigh, her belly quivering at that first deliciously intimate intrusion. She felt each delve and dive of his tongue as it searched every corner of her mouth before mating with her tongue, stabbing at it, stroking it, sucking on it, sweeping over it until she was sagging against him with legs that refused to hold her upright.

His hands moved from the tops of her shoulders to her waist, pulling her closer so she could feel the hard surge of his body against her.

It had been *so* long since she had felt a man's response to her and it both thrilled and terrified her. She wasn't ready for this. This wasn't supposed to be happening. Not now. Not here. Not in Cornwall when she was working on what could turn out to be the biggest case of her career. She was supposed to be in control. She wasn't supposed to go all weak and watery at the knees just because a very attractive man decided he wanted to prove a point. Although he was proving it rather convincingly, she had to admit. Her mouth felt as if someone had set it alight. Fireworks were going off in her head and her body was melting like ice cream left out in the hot midday sun.

His tongue did another round of her mouth, but this time his hands moved from her waist and cupped her bottom and tugged her even closer to his hardness. She had no hope of resisting that little manoeuvre either. She rubbed herself up against him, her inner thighs trembling at the thought of him driving between them and exploding with the blistering passion she could feel was banked up in him.

'I hate to interrupt, but can you do that somewhere else?' Poppy's voice sounded from the doorway leading into the kitchen. 'It's totally gross.'

Eloise sprang out of Lachlan's arms so quickly she almost fell over. She clutched at the nearest surface and steadied herself, but she had no hope of controlling the rapid tide of red-hot colour that stormed into her cheeks.

Lachlan ran a hand through his hair but unlike Eloise he seemed totally at ease with the situation, which made Eloise wonder how many women he'd brought home before.

'I thought you were staying overnight at Fiona's?' he said. 'You should have called and I would have picked you up. I hope you didn't walk home alone.'

'*Da-ad.*' Poppy rolled her eyes. 'I do know how to protect myself, you know.'

'Well, I certainly hope you aren't considering taking self-defence lessons from Dr Hayden,' he quipped, with a teasing glance in Eloise's direction.

Eloise glared back at him. 'You took me by surprise, that's all,' she said hotly.

He gave her a playful grin. 'You didn't even put up a token fight.'

'I didn't want to hurt you,' she said, scowling at him. 'I could have blackened your eye or broken your wrist or something.'

'While you two get on with pretending you're not seriously attracted to each other, I'm going to bed,' Poppy announced.

Lachlan frowned as he noticed how pale his daughter looked. 'Are you all right, sweetheart?' he asked gently.

Poppy's eyes began to water but she quickly brushed at them with the back of her hand. 'I wanted to talk to Mum,' she said. 'I called her earlier but she was busy and hasn't bothered to call me back.'

'Honey, you know how hard she works,' Lachlan said. 'She probably got tied up with some important clients or something.'

'You don't have to pretend with me,' Poppy said churlishly. 'I know you hate her so there's no point in playing the under-standing ex-husband.'

'I do *not* hate your mother,' Lachlan insisted. 'We've been through all this before, Poppy. I know it's hard getting used to living with just me instead of both of us but you have to move on. We both do. Your mother and I are not getting back together. We weren't even together all the years we lived here, not in the real sense.'

'I know…' Poppy's shoulders slumped as she turned away. 'I'm going to bed.'

'You could at least say goodnight to Dr Hayden,' Lachlan said.

'It's fine,' Eloise said. 'Let her be, Chief Inspector.'

Poppy turned to face Eloise. 'You called him Chief Inspector. Don't you know his name?'

'Yes, I do but I—'

'If you're going to sleep with him, you should at least know his first name,' Poppy cut her off rudely.

'I wasn't planning on sleeping with your father,' Eloise said with deliberate firmness. 'I only met him for the first time earlier today.'

'That didn't stop you from kissing him.'

'He kissed me,' Eloise said somewhat defensively. 'I had no intention of—'

'Was he any good?' Poppy cut her off again.

'Poppy, I hardly think—' Lachlan began.

Eloise lifted her chin and held the young girl's challenging brown gaze. 'Yes, he was, actually,' she said. 'Better than good.'

Poppy's eyes went wide. 'Really?'

'Yes,' Eloise answered. 'Up there with the best, actually.'

Poppy turned to her father. 'Are you going to have an affair with her?' she asked.

'I'm seriously considering it,' he answered with a tilt of his mouth.

'Ahem…' Eloise gave them both a pointed look. 'I think I might be the one to decide that.'

'Have you decided?' Poppy asked.

'No, and I don't think I—'

'If you do happen to sleep with my father, don't assume we're going to be best friends or anything,' Poppy said. 'I don't need another mother—I have a perfectly good one of my own.'

'Lucky you,' Eloise said. 'I don't have a mother or a father.'

Poppy's expression visibly softened in contrition. 'Oh… sorry… I didn't realise…'

'It's fine,' Eloise said. 'I learned to accept it a long time ago.'

'You must think I'm a spoilt brat,' Poppy said, shifting from foot to foot.

'I understand that you are dealing with some pretty heavy stuff right now,' Eloise said. 'The divorce of your parents and the unexpected death of an acquaintance is hardly a walk in the park.'

Poppy chewed at her bottom lip without answering, but Eloise observed how the young girl's cheeks had heightened in colour at the mention of Ethan Jenson's death.

Lachlan bent down to kiss his daughter on the cheek. 'I'm just going to walk Dr Hayden back to the guest-house. Will you be OK while I'm gone?'

Tears shone in Poppy's eyes as she looked up at her father. Eloise saw the way the girl's throat moved up and down and the way her body began to tremble.

Lachlan enveloped her in his arms and held her close. 'What is it, Poppy? Has someone upset you? Or hurt you in some way?'

She shook her head against his chest. 'No, I'm just a bit emotional right now. Everyone's talking about Ethan Jenson's death. There are rumours going about that he was murdered.' She lifted her head and looked up at him. 'He wasn't, was he, Dad?'

'You know I can't discuss police business with you, sweetheart,' he said gently. 'But so far the verdict is death by drowning.'

'Drowning is bad enough,' Poppy sniffed. 'But murder is much worse. It means someone is out there who wanted him dead. What if they want someone else dead? Who is going to stop them?'

'Do you want to go and stay with your mother for a few days until things settle down?' he asked.

Poppy gnawed at her bottom lip again, looking more like a child of six than a well-developed sixteen-year-old. 'No,' she said on the back end of a sigh. 'I want to spend some time with Robert. I sort of promised him we'd go on a picnic to the smugglers' caves.'

'I thought you weren't seeing him any more?' Eloise said before she could stop herself.

Poppy frowned as she turned to look at her, her expression colouring again. 'Did he tell you that?'

Eloise nodded. 'Your father and I spoke with him earlier this evening. He had a slight altercation with some youths in the alley behind the Penhally Arms.'

Poppy looked worried. 'Is he all right?'

'He's fine,' Lachlan answered. 'Nick Tremayne had to give him a couple of stitches but apart from that he'll be as good as new in the morning.'

Poppy's shoulders drooped with exhaustion as she headed for the stairs. 'Sorry for disturbing you. You can get back to what you were doing now. I'm going to bed.'

'We weren't doing anything,' Eloise felt compelled to say.

Poppy's mouth stretched into a little smile. 'Maybe I will book in for some self-defence classes with you, Dr Hayden,' she said. 'They look like fun.'

'Go to bed, you obnoxious brat,' Lachlan growled.

Eloise picked up her bag for the second time once Poppy had disappeared upstairs. 'I really must go,' she said. 'Beatrice Trevallyn will think I've come to a perilous end, like the last Australian to visit the village.'

Lachlan opened the door for her. 'Can you swim?' he asked. 'I don't mean the English Channel but enough to save yourself.'

'Of course I can swim,' she answered. 'I can assure you,

Chief Inspector D'Ancey, that I am in absolutely no danger of drowning.'

'That's good to know,' he said as he led the way down the path to the street. 'The last thing this place needs is another accidental death.'

She waited until they had walked a few paces before speaking again. 'Poppy seemed very upset. Do you think it was just about the rumours about Ethan Jenson's death?'

He took a moment to answer. 'I think everyone is upset about Ethan Jenson's death, rumours notwithstanding. The sooner this case is wrapped up, the better.'

Eloise couldn't help thinking he was keen to get rid of her, irrespective of his kiss. It might not take him long to forget about her once she was back in Sydney behind her cluttered desk, but she knew it would very likely take her the rest of her life to forget how it felt to have his mouth on hers.

'About that kiss…' he said into the silence broken only by the whisper of the silvery sea as it stroked against the shore in lace-fringed waves.

'I've forgotten all about it,' she said.

'Liar.'

'You only did it to prove a point.'

'It was extremely enjoyable.'

She turned to glance at him. 'The kiss or proving the point?'

He grinned down at her. 'No harm in a little bit of both, don't you think?'

She narrowed her eyes at him. 'I felt extremely embarrassed in front of your daughter.'

'Don't worry. She's used to it.'

Her disapproving frown increased. 'Used to you proving a point or bringing home strange women and kissing them senseless in your kitchen?'

He stopped and smiled down at her. 'Did I kiss you senseless?'

She pursed her lips. 'I'm not going to answer that.'

He chuckled and began to move on, taking her by the elbow with the cup of his palm. 'If you didn't send out all those sexy signals all the time, I wouldn't dream of kissing you.'

She snorted derisively. 'That is just so typical of men like you. You think because a woman comes over for a drink or a meal it means they want to hop into bed with you. I haven't hopped into bed with a man for longer than I can remember and I'm not going to do it just because you're…you're…'

He grinned down at her. 'I'm what? Single and available?'

'Single and attractive.'

'You think I'm attractive?'

'You know you are,' she said. 'You're tall and dark and handsome. I know it's a cliché but a lot of women really go for that look.'

'Anything else?'

'You care about people—your daughter, for instance. I don't even know who my father is and he's certainly made no effort to find me in the last thirty-two years of my life, so in my book you rate pretty high on the good father monitor.'

'What else?'

She turned to look up at him again. 'You're divorced from your wife but you've never once said a bad word about her. I admire that in a man. So many of the men I've met take every opportunity to vilify their ex-partners.'

'Wow, praise indeed from the uptight Dr Eloise Hayden from Australia.'

She frowned at him. 'You think I'm uptight?'

'I think you need to chill out a little, Eloise,' he said.

'I suppose by chilling out you mean I should have a full-on fling with you while I'm here to make things really interesting.'

His brown eyes twinkled at her. 'It would certainly make things very interesting for the locals.'

'I don't want to be the subject of local gossip.'

'You've definitely come to the wrong place if you want to avoid that,' he said. 'It will be all over the village by morning that we had dinner together. Most people will assume our dinner led to other more satisfying activities.'

She frowned at him sourly. 'Because of your womanising reputation?'

'No,' he said, running his gaze over her stained vest top and close-fitting jeans. 'Because you don't fit the stereotype of the career-woman at all.'

'I look completely different when I'm dressed in a suit.'

'I'd prefer to see you in nothing at all.'

Eloise's jaw dropped open. 'Chief Inspector D'Ancey you are being *highly* inappropriate.'

'I know, but I enjoy seeing you blush,' he said with a teasing smile. 'That was some kiss, though, wasn't it?'

She had to look away from his dancing-with-merriment eyes. 'It was all right, I guess.'

'All right?' He made a sound of affronted pride. 'I gave it my best shot. If Poppy hadn't turned up when she did, I think we might have taken it a step further.'

She gave him a schoolmistress sort of look from beneath her brows. 'You think.'

He gave her a tiny tap on the end of her uptilted nose with one finger. 'I know, Dr Hayden,' he said with a confident smile. 'I know.'

CHAPTER NINE

ELOISE'S INABILITY to fall into a decent sleep had nothing whatsoever to do with her lingering jet-lag, she decided as she tossed and turned till dawn. Lachlan had delivered her to the door of the guest-house and under the cover of darkness had pressed a barely-there kiss to her mouth before leaving her standing there aching for more.

She gave the pillow another hard thump and groaned in frustration. Her lips still felt tingly and her body restless and the sound of Mr Price's laptop computer being pecked at in the early hours of the morning certainly hadn't helped her to relax.

Peck. Peck. Peck. Peck.

It reminded her of Lachlan's pen as he'd sat opposite her…had it really only been a few hours ago? So much seemed to have happened since then.

The pecking of the computer finally stopped and she closed her eyes, willing herself to sleep, when she heard Mr Price speaking into what she assumed was a Dictaphone.

'The killer had stalked the victim relentlessly for months, day and night, like a shadow of evil cast over her, always

there, always invisible but always there. She knew it. She felt it. She sensed it. She even smelt it.'

Eloise buried her head under another pillow and gave another groan.

The County Coroner's Office was located in part of the police headquarters complex in Wadebridge. Eloise had declined Lachlan's offer the night before to drive her there as she wanted to familiarise herself with the area. She also felt the need to re-establish her professional persona. Spending so much time with him the day before had upended her normally rigidly adhered-to priorities.

Dr Peter Middleton, the chief pathologist of Wadebridge County, greeted Eloise as she arrived and introduced her to his assistant, Dr Grant Yates.

'I am sure you have been sent on a bit of a fool's errand, Dr Hayden,' Peter Middleton said as he led the way to the autopsy room. 'I found nothing to suggest anything other than death by drowning.'

'I'm not necessarily here to prove you and Dr Yates wrong,' Eloise said. 'The family deserves to have a second opinion, even if it proves in the end to be the same as yours.'

'I am very sure it will be,' Peter Middleton said with the type of arrogance Eloise loathed seeing in a colleague. 'Morning, Chief Inspector,' he added, as Lachlan peeled himself away from the wall where he had been waiting for them to arrive. 'This is wasting your valuable time as well.'

'That remains to be seen,' Lachlan said, exchanging a quick glance with Eloise.

Eloise pressed her lips together and followed them into the autopsy room where Peter handed them both theatre scrubs.

'You can show Dr Hayden where the change rooms are,' he said to Lachlan.

'Come this way,' Lachlan said and led her to the corridor outside. 'It's the first door on the right. I'll wait for you here.'

Eloise changed into the scrubs and left her things on the hooks behind the door. She allowed herself one quick glance in the mirror and then wished she hadn't. She looked younger than Poppy with no make-up on, her hair flat and her eyes shadowed with tiredness.

She blew out a little breath and went back out to the corridor, where Lachlan was standing dressed in scrubs, again leaning against the wall in that lazy, I've-got-all-the-time-in-the-world manner of his.

'Ready?' he asked, with a little smile of reassurance.

She nodded briskly but inside her stomach was already churning. As much as she loved her work, she hated doing autopsies on young people. It was hard enough doing one on an older person, but when it was someone who hadn't had a chance to live even a quarter of their life it struck at the very heart of her. She felt for the families, the agony of loss they would go through for the rest of their lives, every birthday, every Christmas, and worst of all the anniversary of their loved one's death.

When they re-entered the autopsy room the body had already been wheeled in and placed on a stainless-steel bench in the centre of the room. The overhead lights were switched on, as was the camera to record the autopsy. The microphone Eloise was to use to record her comments was set up and ready to go.

She automatically looked up to the side of the light assembly where a sign in Latin was routinely placed in autopsy rooms across the globe. Somehow it comforted her to find it there.

Hic locus est ubi mors gaudet succurrere vitae. Here a place where death gladly teaches the living.

Around the outside of the room were the usual benches with empty specimen jars, chemical containers, a microscope and a large collection of surgical instruments.

Donning gloves, plastic apron, mask and eye shield, Eloise clicked a button on the floor and started dictating into the overhead microphone, Grant Yates moving forward to help her turn the body as needed.

'External examination,' she began. 'Body of a Caucasian male aged twenty-seven, blonde hair, no external marks of trauma. Incisions from previous autopsy consist of midline thoracoabdominal incision and circumferential scalp incision, both closed with silk sutures. External evidence of prolonged immersion in water from skin wrinkling.'

She took a deep breath and tried to rid her mind of images of that young strong body riding some of the toughest waves the world's oceans could throw up. He had been a good-looking young man, his sun-bleached blond hair, tanned skin and leanly muscled form no doubt a huge drawcard for women across the globe.

She couldn't help wondering if Poppy D'Ancey had indeed experienced a brief fling with him. He had been a lot older than her, of course, but Eloise knew young girls were often attracted to older men. Poppy was a mixture of little girl and sultry siren so it seemed likely Ethan Jenson would have taken what was on offer, in spite of what Lachlan thought.

She looked up to see him watching her, those brown eyes steady on hers, that same reassuring look he'd sent her earlier softening his gaze even more. After their first disastrous encounter she never for one moment would have thought she'd be glad he was here with her. But she was.

'Dr Middleton, I noted from your report that the lungs were full of seawater but that there was no pulmonary oedema from your biopsy. Can you show me from where you took the biopsy?'

The previously removed lungs had been replaced in the thoracic cavity, which was now being spread apart by a retractor inserted by Dr Middleton.

'Yes,' he said. 'From the base of the left lung. There's the incision.'

'Tell me, Dr Middleton, was there anything in the main airways when they were opened?' she asked.

'Seawater, full of seawater, and lots of it.'

'Was there any froth in the airway?' Eloise asked.

In her extensive experience with drowning victims from Australian beaches, usually the victim struggled in the last minutes to get breath. As seawater mixed with mucus in the airway it tended to froth, making breathing even harder and often accelerating the drowning process.

'No froth, just seawater.'

'I wonder if we could take some samples near the end of the bronchi?' she asked. 'I want to see if any foreign material has been aspirated.'

'Foreign material?' Peter Middleton looked at her scathingly. 'What on earth do you think you might find? A school of fish?'

Eloise tightened her mouth without responding and continued with her work. Having taken several more samples of lung tissue for histological examination, she then turned her attention to the diatom testing.

'Dr Middleton, those diatom samples from the lungs— could you tell me how you collected those?' she asked.

'Well, from that briny water in the trachea, of course. I examined them myself. Why, do you think they are wrong?'

'There are a couple of curious features about them, that's all,' she replied, trying to be polite in spite of his brusque manner. 'Did you prepare the sample yourself for microscopy?'

There was a small pause before he answered. 'No, as a matter of fact, I think in this case one of the *deiners*—Michael, I think it was, may have got the samples ready. He's unfortunately not with us now. His mother, who lives in Canada, had a stroke and he's taken leave.'

'Well, from your description of the diatoms, it seems like there may have been freshwater contamination of the samples, maybe from washing or some other slip-up in sample preparation. I'd like to try and get more of that water out of the lungs, and also take a range of samples from other body tissues for diatom analysis. And I'd also like to do a quantitative analysis. Chief Inspector D'Ancey is organising some samples from the drowning site for comparison.'

Eloise looked up at that point and found Lachlan's gaze on her. He gave her a glimmer of a smile as if to reassure her.

She turned back to the body of the young man and began taking multiple tissue samples from several organs. She then worked with Peter Middleton and his assistant to prepare slides and the diatom samples for microscopy, all under her direct supervision.

In addition, she collected blood from the inferior vena cava for carbon monoxide analysis. The lab possessed a gas analyser, so all the testing could be completed within a few days.

Finally the body was sewn back together, using basketball stitch, and returned to the drawer where it had been stored.

'Time for a break,' Peter Middleton said, stripping off his

gloves. 'Grant, can you organise some coffee? I just need to make a couple of calls.'

Lachlan came over to where Eloise was tidying up. 'How are you holding up?' he asked.

She straightened her shoulders. 'I'm perfectly fine. Why do you ask?'

'You looked upset.'

'I can assure you I'm not.'

'Then you should be,' he said. 'Every death is upsetting, none more so than when it's a young person.'

'I seem to remember you saying last night that police officers had to remain clinically detached, or words to that effect,' she said stubbornly, refusing to show that she was indeed feeling emotionally drained.

'You can't shut down completely, Eloise,' he said. 'It's neither healthy nor normal.'

She gave him a direct look. 'So you're admitting to shedding a tear or two behind your mask for Ethan Jenson, are you?'

'I'm admitting that death in a young person is always a tragedy, no matter who they are,' he said. 'Have you arranged to meet his parents yet?'

'No, they haven't requested it so I thought I would wait until the results are in.'

'They will want to see you well before that, Dr Hayden,' he said, and turned away, leaving her standing there alone with the scent of death lingering in the air.

Eloise spent an hour with Ethan Jenson's parents at their request the following day, her heart aching for what they were going through. The pain of their loss was etched on their faces, their eyes red and swollen from endless crying and their cheeks hollowed out with anguish. She expressed her sympathy and did her best to reassure them that the tests she had conducted would hopefully provide them with some sort of closure during such a harrowing time.

'Thank you for coming all this way,' Hugh Jenson said as Eloise prepared to leave. 'We really appreciate the effort you've made to find out the truth about our son's death.'

Eloise took each of their hands in turn. 'As soon as we find out the results of the tests, the chief inspector will contact you,' she said. 'It may take another day or two. I'm sorry you've had to wait so long. I know how hard it makes it, having things drawn out like this.'

'We just want to know the truth,' Jeanne Jenson said, wiping at her eyes. 'I know Ethan wasn't an angel but people are saying things about him that are very upsetting. I won't be able to rest until I know for sure if someone…you know…' she choked over another sob '…did away with him.'

Eloise spent the next few days exploring the local countryside as she waited for the lab tests to be processed. She didn't hear from Lachlan, although she saw him once or twice in the distance, talking to one of the local fishermen by the harbour. On one occasion he lifted his hand in a wave when he caught her staring at him but she quickly turned on her heel and pretended she hadn't seen him. She felt she needed these few days to make some sort of sense of the ambiguity of her feelings towards him and it would only confuse her even more to spend time interacting with him. But avoiding him only made her think of him all the more. She lay awake at night, listening to the pecking of Mr Price in the room next door, and wondered what Lachlan was doing. She walked along the sandy shore each day, listening to the smacking and sucking of the waves, and wondered if he was thinking of how her mouth had felt beneath the heated pressure of his.

Stop it, she remonstrated as she stomped back towards the café on the Harbour Front at the end of the week. She had to stop thinking about a man who was probably just toying with her for a bit of fun. What could he offer her in terms of a relationship anyway? He lived on the opposite side of the globe, for one thing, and the other was…well, she didn't want to fall in love with anyone, much less a recently divorced single dad who had a troubled teenager on his hands.

She had not long been served her coffee when she looked up and saw Poppy come into the café with a friend.

Poppy's red-rimmed eyes briefly met Eloise's gaze before falling away. She murmured something to the girl beside her then they both turned around and left without so much as a greeting.

Eloise could understand Lachlan's reluctance to have his young daughter involved in this case, and while she understood the protocol that prevented her from interviewing witnesses or suspects, she couldn't help sensing something was amiss and would have loved a quiet moment or two—off the record—with the chief inspector's daughter.

Her mobile phone rang just as she drained the last of her coffee and Peter Middleton's voice informed her, 'I have the results from Forensics Services, Dr Hayden. They came in a few moments ago. I thought you might like to meet me at the lab and see them for yourself.'

An hour or so later, Eloise looked up from her microscope. Peter Middleton was sitting next to her, still looking down the second eyepiece of the lab microscope.

'Well, Dr Hayden, this certainly changes things, doesn't it?' he said after a moment.

'It appears so, Dr Middleton,' she said. 'What we have here

now are clear signs of foul play. The diatom test is negative for all tissues, only positive for the water in the lungs. There is clearly foreign matter, looking remarkably like feathers, in the peripheral airways, and the carbon monoxide levels are very high. I would say Ethan Jenson was well and truly dead by the time he hit the water—dead from a combination of smothering and carbon monoxide. He was in the water for at least six hours, but he didn't die from drowning. I'd say he was put into the water about midnight, if he was found around six a.m. the next morning.'

Dr Middleton took off his glasses and leaned back in his chair, his normally curt, no-nonsense manner disappearing completely. 'I guess I have an apology to make.'

'You don't need to apologise, Dr Middleton,' Eloise said with a gracious smile. 'I've had this same experience myself. You make unconscious assumptions and do what seem to be the appropriate investigations—they lead to what seem like reasonable conclusions and then someone comes in from outside, takes a fresh look, and says, "What about this or that?" and suddenly your assumptions look shaky. We've had some famous cases in Australia that have blown up on the basis of external reviews of the evidence, leading to charges being laid or, in one notorious case, a quashed conviction.'

'Well, it looks like this case has just "blown up", as you put it. I appreciate your review, and the fresh angles you've provided,' he said. He gave an audible sigh and confessed, 'On reflection, I feel I should have conducted far more extensive tests in the first place. We usually do with anyone high profile, but there had been a nasty vehicle accident the day before. A hit and run…' He wiped his forehead with his handkerchief and shifted his eyes away from hers.

'I understand how difficult it is,' Eloise said softly.

'Forensic Services are under constant pressure to produce results in a hurry. It's the same back home.'

Peter Middleton's gaze went back to the two signed copies of laboratory results in front of them. 'The family will need to be informed and Chief Inspector D'Ancey,' he said in a weighted tone.

'Yes.'

'I'll take you to his office,' he said, getting to his feet. 'It's a short walk from here.'

Eloise followed him out of the laboratory, wondering what Lachlan was going to say when he heard what she had uncovered.

Lachlan stared at his daughter in shock. 'Are you sure?' he asked, 'absolutely, totally, without a doubt sure?'

Poppy nodded miserably. 'I saw Dr Tremayne a few days ago. He confirmed it. I'm six…' She gulped and continued, 'Almost seven weeks along.'

Lachlan let out a stiff curse and then, seeing the crestfallen look on his daughter's face, came around to where she was sitting and gathered her in his arms.

'I'm so sorry, Dad,' she choked. 'I don't know how I'm going to tell Mum. It's taken me all this time to tell you. I know she'll kill me.'

Lachlan swallowed back his emotion. 'No, she won't,' he said. 'We'll talk to her together and discuss your options.'

Poppy lifted her head away from his chest and looked up at him. 'You mean…get rid of it?'

He swallowed deeply again. 'If that is what you decide to do then I will support you through it,' he said. 'But I don't want you to rush into anything you might later regret. There's a lot to take into consideration—your age, for one thing. I know you feel all grown up, sweetheart, but you're still a child yourself.'

'I know…' she gulped again, and fumbled for a tissue.

Lachlan handed her his handkerchief. His chest felt tight at the sound of her blowing her nose. That simple action reminded him of the hundreds of times over the years he had mopped her tears as a little girl.

But she was no longer a little girl.

She was going to be a mother.

Margaret was going to kill *him*, not Poppy, he thought with a sickening clench of his insides. He should have been more vigilant in checking she was on the Pill, but he had foolishly thought his ex-wife had seen to that.

'Have you told Robert?' he asked once Poppy had stopped sniffing.

'No…I c-can't…' She began to cry all over again.

He frowned and reached for her again, tipping up her chin like he'd been doing ever since she'd been a toddler. 'Why not, Poppy? Surely he has the right to know?'

Her slim throat moved up and down in anguish. 'Because I—I'm not sure if it's his…'

It took Lachlan a good ten seconds or more to register what she had just said. He stood staring down at her, his heart beginning to thud unevenly as a thought crept into his mind like a shadow slipping underneath a door.

'Who else's could it be?' he asked in a cracked whisper that sounded nothing like his normal voice.

She looked at him through tear-glazed eyes and said, 'Ethan Jenson's.'

CHAPTER TEN

THE intercom suddenly buzzed on Lachlan's desk. 'Yes?' he clipped out.

'There's a Dr Eloise Hayden here to see you,' the junior constable said. 'Shall I send her in?'

'Can you ask her to wait a minute or two?' he asked, looking at Poppy who was still pale and trembling.

'Will do.'

Lachlan shoved a hand through his hair as he came back to where his daughter was standing. 'Do you want me to tell your mother for you?' he asked gently.

She bit her lip. 'I want to tell her myself. I phoned her earlier and asked her to come and pick me up and take me back with her for a few days. She was a bit iffy to start with but then she agreed to meet me this afternoon here in Wadebridge. You don't mind, do you, Dad?'

'No, not at all,' he said thinking of the very intuitive Eloise Hayden sniffing around. The sooner Poppy was out of town, the better. 'Have you told anyone else—one of your friends, for instance?'

She shook her head. 'No, only you and Dr Tremayne know. He insisted I tell you.'

'Good. Let's keep it that way for now,' he said. After a little pause he added, 'Did you have strong feelings for Ethan or was it just a little fling to make Robert sit up and take notice?'

Poppy gave him a shamefaced look. 'It was a stupid mistake to get involved with him,' she said. 'I was trying to make Robert jealous after we had that horrible argument a few weeks back. Ethan flirted with me and I enjoyed the attention but then it sort of got out of hand.'

Lachlan felt every hair on the back of his neck lift in apprehension. 'He didn't force you, did he?'

'No, of course not,' she answered glumly. 'I was just too stupid to see him for what he is…I mean was. He slept with three other girls that same week, including Molly Beale of all people. She's so slutty. I feel disgusted with myself for falling for his charm like that.'

He gave her shoulder a gentle squeeze. 'We all make mistakes, sweetheart,' he said.

'I'm so sorry, Dad,' she said again. 'You must be so disappointed in me.'

He pressed a soft kiss to the top of her head. 'I'm disappointed in myself for not seeing the potential for this happening. I feel I've let you down by not protecting you. I guess I've been too distracted, dealing with the divorce.'

'It's not your fault,' she said. 'I know you and Mum weren't happy together. I've known it for years. I've been such a pain, I'm sorry. I just wanted Mum to put me first for once.'

'She does her best,' he said. 'It's been hard for her. She didn't really want to be tied down with a husband and child so young.'

'What about you?' she asked. 'Did you ever resent me being born?'

He smiled at her tenderly. 'What sort of question is that? Of course I haven't resented or regretted it, not for a moment. You are my daughter and I can't imagine life without you.'

She smiled a watery smile and reached up to plant a kiss on his cheek. 'I'd better get going. The bus will be here any minute and I don't want to miss Mum. You know how impatient she is.'

'Do you want me to wait with you? My meeting with Dr Hayden won't take long.'

Poppy gave him a probing look. 'Are you falling for her, Dad?'

He looked at her incredulously. 'In a little over a week? Don't be ridiculous.'

'She's very attractive.'

'She's also very career-driven.'

'I think she likes you.'

'Yes, well, she's going to hate me if she finds out just how involved you were with Ethan Jenson and that I deliberately withheld the information from her,' he said with a deepening frown.

'You're not going to tell her, are you?'

He let out a sigh. 'Not right now, no.'

'Will you get into big trouble, Dad?'

Lachlan looked at his daughter's anxious face and let out another sigh. 'Not if I can help it.' He opened the door and led her out. 'Come on, sweetheart. I'll walk you to the back entrance.'

'He's free now,' the constable informed Eloise a few minutes later. 'It's the first door on the left.'

'Thank you,' Eloise said, and made her way to where she had been directed.

She gave the door a single knock and he issued a command to come in. He was sitting behind his desk, a mound of paperwork on either side of him, but he rose to his feet as she came in.

'I take it you've received the results?' he asked.

'Yes.'

He couldn't help being pleased to see her, but Lachlan didn't like the sound of that curt one-word answer. 'Take a seat,' he said, and once she had sat down he resumed his own seat behind the desk, forcing himself not to reach for his pen to click.

He schooled his features into indifference and asked, 'What did you find?'

'Ethan Jenson was murdered, Chief Inspector,' she stated bluntly. 'He was dead before he hit the water, a combination of smothering and carbon-monoxide poisoning. Feather particles were found in the lung biopsies I took.'

He leaned back in his chair and began to drum his fingers on the desk. 'The family will have to be informed at some point.'

'Yes,' she said. 'And everyone who knew or was associated with Mr Jenson will have to be interviewed. Chief Inspector, that includes your daughter.'

His eyes hardened as they held hers. 'How many times do I have to tell you she has nothing to do with any of this?'

'Are you saying that because you hope it's true or because you're absolutely certain?'

'My daughter is not capable of murder.'

'Perhaps not, but one of her friends or acquaintances could be,' she pointed out. 'As far as I'm concerned, she's a valuable witness for this investigation.'

He shook his head. 'Looking at the criteria you're using, just about everybody in the whole of Cornwall would be just as valuable.'

'You're obviously too close to the investigation to make rational decisions,' she said. 'I'm going to suggest to the superintendent that you step aside and let someone else take charge.'

His expression darkened. 'That won't be necessary. I'm

heading this investigation, Dr Hayden and no one else. I'll make sure all avenues are investigated. Do you understand?'

She lifted her chin. 'And I want to be informed of each and every development along the way, have you got that?'

He got to his feet. 'You will be notified of anything of significance as per standard procedure. You know the angle we take on this. If we go out to the community and suddenly announce to all and sundry that Jenson was murdered, the culprit will know we're on to him and disappear into the woodwork.'

'I realise the delicacy needed in handling cases such as this. It's always a bit of a balancing act,' she said.

The intercom buzzed on Lachlan's desk again and he turned back to lean over his desk to answer it. 'Yes?'

'Chief, Dr Tremayne called a few moments ago. He said he was going to be ten minutes late.'

Lachlan felt a tremor of unease pass through him. 'Oh…right… Give me a buzz when he arrives. Dr Hayden is just leaving.'

Eloise looked at him quizzically. 'Getting rid of me, Chief Inspector? What if I want to speak to Dr Tremayne about my findings?'

'You can book an appointment with him some other time. This is a personal visit.'

'And yet you sounded surprised to know he was coming here,' she observed.

'Did I?' he asked guilelessly.

'Yes.'

'I forgot he said he might be dropping past.'

'Just like you forgot which day it was you were supposed to take your daughter to her friend's house?' she questioned.

He sent her a disarming smile. 'Not much escapes your notice, does it?'

'Not if I can help it.'

He came to stand right in front of her. 'Well, then, clever little Dr Hayden from Australia, maybe I'm just a little forgetful sometimes. Or perhaps I'm distracted by the fact I am struggling to keep my hands off you,' he said in a low sexy drawl.

Eloise felt her body quiver in reaction. She looked up into those brown eyes and felt that cold and hard feeling she'd carried inside her chest for so long melt, its warmth flowing through each and every one of her veins. Her heartbeat increased, her mouth began to tingle and her belly flip-flopped as he came one step closer. 'Um…you're changing the subject…' she said, running her tongue across her lips. 'I didn't notice…er…that…'

He picked up a strand of her hair and looped it around his finger. 'Can we meet up later tonight?' he asked. 'Say about nine?'

'I'm not sure I should say yes,' she said, still staring at his mouth. 'I mean, I'm not really sure what I'm saying yes to.'

'How about we have a walk along the shore and take things from there?' he suggested.

She looked back into his eyes and felt her normally rigid resolve melt and slip away even further. 'Is it wise for us to do that?'

Lachlan took a moment to answer. Of course it wasn't wise, certainly not now with things as they were, but something about Eloise pulled him like a magnet. In spite of the danger she represented, he wanted to have her, even if it was only for a few weeks. He wanted to break through that tough exterior she carried around like a suit of armour and have her purring like a sensual cat instead. She was a passionate woman—he could feel it every time he looked at her or touched her.

'Are you worried about what people might say?' he asked.

'To some degree, yes,' she said. 'I like to keep my private life private. I guess that's hard to do in a small village like this.'

Tell me about it, Lachlan thought wryly. How he was going to keep his daughter's teenage pregnancy quiet for as long as possible was already starting to worry him. Although things had changed over the years, there were still some conservative members of the community who would shun her, which would make a difficult situation intolerable.

'It is hard but not impossible,' he said. 'Anyway, people will expect us to spend time together as part of the investigation.'

'What about your daughter?' she asked.

'What about her?'

'Will you tell her you're…you know…seeing me?'

'*Are* you seeing me, Dr Hayden from Australia?' he asked with another one of his irresistible smiles.

She screwed up her mouth at him. 'Must you keep calling me that?'

'Eloise, then.'

'That's better.'

'Your turn.'

She looked at him in confusion. 'My turn for what?'

'For saying my name,' he said. 'You can't keep calling me Chief Inspector, especially if we end up in bed together.'

'I didn't say I was going to sleep with you,' she said through prim lips.

'You didn't have to,' he said. 'I can see it in your eyes. You want me just as much as I want you. It's called sexual chemistry.'

She gave him one of her prudish schoolmistress-type looks. 'That's nonsense.'

He smiled and opened the door for her. 'I'll meet you at Trevallyn House at nine.'

She sent him a pert glance as she brushed past him in the doorway. 'What if I change my mind?'

'That's entirely up to you,' he said. 'Just give me a call to let me know.'

Eloise wasn't so sure she liked his take-it-or-leave-it attitude. 'I might get a better offer,' she said, with a haughty lift of her chin.

'You might but then again you might not.' His eyes twinkled. 'You know what they say about a bird in the hand and all that.'

Eloise left with a roll of her eyes, but his chuckle filled her head for the remainder of the afternoon, and every time she looked at her watch the hands seemed to be crawling at a snail's pace towards nine p.m.

CHAPTER ELEVEN

'POPPY told me her news,' Lachlan said gravely as soon as Nick Tremayne sat down in his office. 'I can tell you I'm not looking forward to Margaret finding out. Poppy's going back to London with her as we speak.'

'Margaret's not the only one who needs to know,' Nick said. 'Dr Hayden should be informed as well.'

Lachlan jerked upright in his chair. 'No. No way.'

Nick frowned. 'You're not going to tell her?'

'I don't want Poppy's name dragged through the mud. She's just a kid, for God's sake.'

'Peter Middleton spoke to me on the way in,' Nick said. 'Off the record, of course, but as I was the attending doctor he thought I should know the change of verdict. I think you have a professional responsibility to tell Dr Hayden that your daughter had an intimate relationship with Ethan Jenson and that as a result of that relationship she is now pregnant.'

'You seem convinced it is Jenson's baby,' Lachlan said.

'We won't know with any certainty unless we conduct a paternity test. Poppy will have to decide if she wants to know for sure but there are risks involved.'

'What sort of risks?'

'Miscarriage, for one,' Nick answered. 'There's only about a one per cent chance but it still needs to be considered.'

Lachlan shoved a hand through his hair. 'I know it may come across as unfeeling, but right now a miscarriage is sounding pretty good to me.'

'Yes, well, I can understand how you feel and I have discussed Poppy's options with her, but the final decision will have to be hers,' Nick said. 'She will need both yours and Margaret's support during this difficult time.'

'I realise that. That's why I want her kept out of the spotlight until this all dies down.'

'You realise this puts me in a difficult position, don't you?' Nick asked. 'I can't breach patient confidentiality by disclosing Poppy's condition to Dr Hayden. That is your job as her father and Chief Inspector heading the investigation.'

'I will tell her when I think she needs to know,' Lachlan said. 'I just want some time to get my head around it all.'

'She's coming to the clinic at six this evening to see me,' Nick said. 'Do you have any leads on who might be responsible for Jenson's murder?'

Lachlan rubbed his hand over his face in weariness. 'No, but if Dr Hayden hears my daughter's pregnant by the victim she's going to put me right at the top of that list, isn't she?'

Nick narrowed his eyes. 'You're not responsible, though, are you?'

Lachlan scowled at him. 'You know me better than that, Nick. I'm one of the good guys, remember?'

Nick gave him a rare smile. 'Sorry. Had to ask.'

'It's OK. I would have asked you the same question if the tables were turned.' He let out a heavy sigh and, leaning forward, put his head in his hands. 'God I just wish this would all go away.'

'It's a nasty business, that's for sure,' Nick agreed.

Lachlan lifted his head and leaned back in his chair. 'So how are things with you and Kate these days?'

Nick frowned. 'That was a bit out of left field. What makes you ask?'

'Eloise Hayden picked up some sort of a vibe when she was talking to Kate at the clinic. She asked me if you and Kate were an item.'

'Kate and I are friends, as we have been for years,' Nick said. 'You know that.'

Lachlan gave a little shrug. 'I wouldn't have asked but from what I've seen so far, Eloise is pretty switched on.'

'So you're on a first-name basis with her now, are you?' Nick asked. 'Does this mean there's something going on between the two of you?'

'I'm more than thinking about it,' Lachlan admitted. 'I haven't felt like this about anyone before, not even Margaret in the early days.'

'It's about time you put the divorce behind you,' Nick said. 'Although I can't help thinking you're asking for trouble, getting involved with an international colleague. Long-distance relationships never work and you couldn't get much further away than Australia.'

'Don't worry, Nick, I'm not going to fall in love with her,' Lachlan said, although he wondered if was being entirely honest with his friend or even himself.

Nick got to his feet. 'You know what they say about tempting fate.'

Lachlan smiled wryly. 'You're starting to sound like me, rattling off well-worn adages all the time.'

'Yes, well, don't say I didn't warn you.'

'She's a career-woman, Nick. Been there, done that and packed away the T-shirt long ago.'

Nick glanced at his watch. 'I'd better get moving. I've got to call in on Henry Ryall before I head back to the clinic. It sounds like a strep throat.'

'James Derrey was out there yesterday, investigating an alleged theft.'

Nick's brows rose. 'Alleged?'

Lachlan gave a nod. 'Henry's lonely. He's looking for excuses for company.'

'I haven't got the time to waste on people who aren't unwell when I have so many to deal with who are,' Nick growled.

'A cup of tea and a stale biscuit won't hurt you,' Lachlan said. 'If I didn't have this case hanging over my head, I'd go out there myself.'

'You know, you might want to think about having a little chat to Robert Polgrean,' Nick said as he strode towards the door. 'If anyone has a motive for getting rid of Ethan Jenson, it's him.'

Lachlan frowned. 'I will interview everyone I think is connected to the case, but Robert already has a rock-solid alibi for the night in question. I checked that out days ago.'

Nick frowned again. 'But I thought you were convinced it was a simple case of drowning. Why did you feel the need to check out Robert's movements that night?'

'I've been in this business long enough to know things are not always as they seem,' Lachlan said. 'Until Peter Middleton announced his verdict of death by drowning, I was keeping an open mind.'

'Kate told me Dr Hayden was concerned about your reluctance to do another autopsy.'

'Come on, Nick, you've met the victim's parents,' Lachlan said. 'I know they were the ones behind the request but I didn't want to put them through any more agony unless it was absolutely necessary.'

'Have you told them yet?'

'Not yet.'

'They're going to be devastated.'

'Yes, I know,' Lachlan said, sending his hand back through his hair again. 'Drowning is hard enough to accept, but murder is another thing entirely.'

Eloise smiled at Sue, the receptionist at the clinic. 'Hello, Sue, I know I'm a bit early for my meeting with Dr Tremayne but I thought I'd come along anyway.'

'That's fine, Dr Hayden,' Sue said. 'Dr Tremayne is on his way back from a house call but it might be ten or fifteen minutes before he returns. But Kate Althorp is upstairs in Chloe the midwife's office, if you'd rather wait there. Chloe's doing a home visit so you won't be disturbed. I'll let Kate know you are here.'

Eloise waited while Sue contacted Kate via the intercom and within half a minute Kate came downstairs to meet her. 'Has your luggage arrived yet?' she asked as she led the way upstairs. 'Bea told me about your little hiccup.'

'No. Can't you tell?' Eloise said ruefully, as she pointed to the very basic outfit she had bought at St Piran a couple of days previously. 'I called the airline a short time ago. Thankfully they've located it and are shipping it by courier, but I'm not sure when it's going to arrive.'

'I can lend you some things to tide you over,' Kate said as she opened the office door. 'I'm a bit taller than you but I have a few things that might do. I'll bring them round or, even better, you could come to my place for dinner in a day or two. Jem would like to meet you. He's very fond of Lachlan. He thinks it's really cool to be a police officer.'

'I used to think that until I started working alongside the

force,' Eloise admitted wryly. 'Now I sometimes wonder why I put my hand up.'

Kate smiled. 'I feel the same about this place. Nick can be so demanding. I've felt like walking out many times, I can tell you.'

'So why do you stay?'

Kate gave a little shrug. 'I care about the patients…and Nick, of course…'

Eloise let the little silence continue, knowing from years of observing police at work that confessions usually followed.

Kate looked up from the papers she was pretending to be rearranging on the desk. 'I've loved him for years. He's the only man I've ever loved in the true sense of the word.'

'What about your late husband?' Eloise asked.

Kate sighed. 'I loved James in the way you would love a close friend or brother. I knew I couldn't have Nick. He fell in love with Annabel on the first day of university. They had to get married when she became pregnant with their twins. I settled for James and loved him in my way. He was a good man. I missed him terribly when he died but he wasn't the love of my life. My soul mate, if you like.'

'Does such a thing exist?' Eloise didn't realise she had asked out loud what she had been thinking until Kate answered.

'I believe so. Although having said that, I still think you can find someone with similar goals and morals and have a pretty decent life together, but love that lasts a lifetime is rare and it's worth waiting for.'

Eloise felt inclined to agree with her but didn't say so. She was still trying to make sense of her totally uncharacteristic reaction to Lachlan. He affected her like no other man had ever done. She could barely think when she was near him; her body seemed to be on high alert, cutting off the circuit to her brain and every gram of rationality she possessed. She didn't feel like a career-focused professional woman around him, more like a love-struck young girl.

Kate gave her a smile of embarrassment. 'Listen to me,' she said self-deprecatingly. 'It must be peri-menopausal hormones or something.'

'Please, don't apologise,' Eloise said sincerely. 'I feel honoured you felt safe enough to share your feelings with me.'

'I'm not usually the share-my-heart type. I guess it's because you're such a good listener. I sense that you are a deeply sensitive person, Dr Hayden.'

'Please, call me Eloise.'

'Eloise. It's such a pretty name. Does anyone ever shorten it to Ellie?'

'No,' Eloise said. 'Only my mother called me that and since she died I can't quite cope with anyone else doing so. It seems silly really, seeing as was so long ago.'

'The loss of your mother is a huge hurdle to overcome, especially in a woman's life,' Kate said. 'Is your father still alive?'

'I have no idea,' Eloise said. 'I've never met him. I'm not even sure my mother knew who he was.'

Kate suddenly tensed and shifted her gaze slightly. 'How have you dealt with that over the years?'

'I've just accepted it,' Eloise said with an indifferent shrug. 'My mother was pretty loose with her morals. I'm not even sure I would want to know who my father was, to tell you the truth.'

Kate turned to face her. 'Do you think every father—no matter who he is—deserves the right to know he has fathered a child, even if he had no idea at the time it had happened?'

'I guess I do in principle, but what if telling the father was going to be destructive to the child or even to the mother?' she asked. 'I think it's one of those case-by-case scenarios where individuals have to decide what is the best course of action, given the circumstances.'

'What would you do if you found you were pregnant?' Kate asked.

'That would entirely depend on who I was pregnant by,' Eloise answered. 'If I felt the man was to be trusted as a worthy father to my child, I would tell him.'

'What if by telling him you would be threatening his relationships with everyone he held dear?' Kate asked.

Eloise thought about it for a moment, thought too about why Kate was asking such pointed questions. Perhaps she knew someone who was facing exactly that dilemma. Penhally Bay was a small community, the medical practice was busy and Kate had at one time been the practice manager. She would have intimate knowledge of everyone's ailments and circumstances.

'I think I would try and do the right thing by the child and the father,' Eloise answered. 'If my child would benefit from knowing who his or her father was, I would definitely tell him. After, all it's his child, wanted or not.'

Kate let out a sigh. 'You're right, of course. I've thought the same for years but still…'

'Are these questions hypothetical or personal?' Eloise asked after a tiny pause.

Kate met her gaze. 'Personal.'

'I see.'

Another little silence passed.

Kate got to her feet and looked out of the window, her arms crossed in front her chest. 'I want to tell him but I don't know how to go about doing so. You know…bringing up the subject.'

'Do you mean with your son or his father?'

'Both.'

Eloise let another small silence slip by before she asked, 'So what you're saying is your husband wasn't Jem's father?'

Kate slowly turned around to face her. 'James was sub-fertile. We didn't tell anyone about it in the village. We went to London to see a specialist when I failed to fall pregnant. We were both checked out but when the results came back James was devastated, as any man would be. He would have loved a child, a son in particular, but it wasn't to be.'

'But being sub-fertile doesn't mean totally unfertile,' Eloise pointed out. 'The chances of a pregnancy are much lower, of course, but it could have still happened.'

Kate shook her head. 'I know Jem is not James's son. I've known it from the beginning.'

'And you have no doubt who the actual father is?'

'I have no doubt at all.'

'It's Nick Tremayne, isn't it?' Eloise asked.

Kate nodded, anguish clearly written on her features. 'We had one brief…time together…the night of the storm. It should never have happened. We were both in a highly charged emotional state and I let my heart rule my head. Nick did, too, if it comes to that. We've had trouble speaking of that night since…I mean the intimate part of it. We both felt so guilty and ashamed of what we did that ever since we've both tried to pretend it didn't happen. We've been carrying on as we always have—as friends. But a few weeks ago that all changed. Nick finally brought the subject up, only I was so shocked I didn't take the opportunity to talk to him about it like I should have done.'

'What has stopped you telling him Jem is his?' Eloise asked.

'You've met Nick,' Kate said with a rueful set to her features. 'He's not exactly the easiest person to talk to at times. I've wanted to tell him for years but I'm frightened it will destroy the friendship we have. We've known each other since we were teenagers. I'm the one he turns to when he has issues with his kids or the practice. I don't want to jeopardise that.'

'You're going to have to discuss it some time or other,' Eloise advised. 'Your son is nine now but as he grows older he may begin to look more and more like his father. What if Nick somehow guesses it for himself?'

All of a sudden Kate's expression became stricken as the shadow of two large feet appeared at her closed door. Her face paled as she put a trembling hand up to her throat and whispered, 'Oh, no…'

There was a brisk knock and Nick's curt tone clipped out, 'Kate? Have you got Dr Hayden with you?'

Kate's throat moved up and down, making her reply come out slightly strangled. 'Y-yes I have.'

The door opened and Eloise saw the livid expression on Nick Tremayne's face, which meant he must have overhead part if not all of their conversation. The blistering glare he sent in Kate's direction more or less confirmed it.

He turned to Eloise. 'I'm free to see you now, but briefly,' he said crisply. 'I have another rather urgent issue to deal with, as I am sure you'll understand.'

'Yes, yes, of course,' Eloise replied, with a quick glance in Kate's direction.

Kate returned her look with an apprehensive grimace, sat back down at the desk and shuffled some papers with hands that weren't quite steady.

Nick was already striding away, barking at Eloise to follow him downstairs.

He closed the door of his room a few moments later and frowned at her from behind his desk. 'Chief Inspector D'Ancey has already informed me of your findings. I hope you're not going to accuse me of incompetence because I failed to correctly identify the cause of death.'

'No, of course not,' she said. 'Anyway, it wasn't your responsibility in this case to declare the cause of death. You did nothing wrong. Under the circumstances it would be easy to assume he died as a result of drowning.'

He scraped a hand through his salt-and-pepper hair. 'What I just overheard downstairs...' he said, as he levelled his gaze at her. 'I must insist you refrain from discussing it with anyone in Penhally Bay.'

'Of course,' she said. 'How much did you hear of my conversation with Kate?'

His eyes were still blazing with anger and Eloise didn't envy Kate's next meeting with him. 'I am not prepared to discuss or have my private life discussed with virtual strangers,' he bit out.

'If Jem is your son, he needs to know it, and soon,' she said. 'He deserves to know the truth.'

Nick looked at her and gave her a twisted smile, but there was no trace of humour in it. 'You know Lachlan D'Ancey was right about you,' he said. 'You're not just a pretty face.'

Eloise could feel her face growing warm. 'I'm only here for the duration of the investigation,' she said. 'I wouldn't want anyone to get any wrong ideas about Chief Inspector D'Ancey and myself.'

'He's a good man, Dr Hayden. He needs some support right now, especially with this situation with his d—'

Eloise tilted her head quizzically at his abrupt cutting off of his sentence. 'What situation, Dr Tremayne?'

Nick looked at her for a second or two beat before continuing, 'His divorce. It hit him hard. It came right out of the blue.'

'I understood from Chief Inspector D'Ancey that his

divorce was a mutual decision they had been considering for years. He told me that himself.'

Nick Tremayne glanced at his watch and got to his feet. 'Is that all, Dr Hayden?' he asked. 'I need to speak to Kate and I have several patients to see before I go home for the day.'

Eloise rose from her chair. 'That will be all, Dr Tremayne.' She paused then added, 'For now.'

CHAPTER TWELVE

'YOUR luggage has arrived!' Beatrice announced excitedly as soon as Eloise got back to the guest-house. 'Davey's just this minute taken it upstairs to your room.'

'That's the best news I've heard all day,' Eloise said with a relieved sigh.

Beatrice bustled over to the hall table and picked up a sheaf of papers tied with string. 'Oh, and Mr Price left this for you.' She handed it to her. 'It's his manuscript. It's ever so kind of you to offer to read it for him.'

I didn't exactly offer, Eloise thought as she took the thick wad of paper with a strained smile. 'Thanks. I'll read it tonight.'

'Not going out this evening, then?'

'I might go for a walk later,' Eloise said, holding the papers to her chest. 'I have some paperwork to see to first.'

Beatrice checked that no one was about before leaning closer. 'I heard a rumour that you found out that young man didn't drown after all. Is it true?'

Eloise was momentarily taken aback. As far as she knew, the parents of the victim hadn't been formally informed so how anyone else had found out was completely beyond her. 'Where did you hear that?' she asked.

'At the hairdresser's,' Beatrice said. 'Vicki Clements told

me there were suspicious findings to do with the case. She heard one of the other clients talking about it. I think someone the client knows works in the police station at Wadebridge.'

'I'm not at liberty to discuss my findings with anyone other than the police investigating the case.'

'I suppose you mean Chief Inspector D'Ancey,' Beatrice said. 'Davey said he saw you and the chief inspector down at the Penhally Arms the other night.'

Eloise felt like sinking through the ancient floorboards. It seemed that Davey Trevallyn saw a great deal and yet she still hadn't met him. 'We were discussing official business,' she said. 'We have to work together on this case.'

There was a footfall on the stairs and a bulky man in his middle to late forties appeared, his round cheeks and innocent, childlike look immediately identifying him as Beatrice's son, Davey.

'Ah, Davey, my love, finally you get to meet our important guest,' Beatrice said. 'This is Dr Hayden. You remember I told you about her coming all this way from Australia to find out the truth about that surfer's death?'

Davey blinked once or twice and mumbled something in reply, but Eloise couldn't understand a word of it.

'Don't be shy,' Beatrice scolded him fondly. 'I know you don't like meeting strangers but Dr Hayden's a nice lady. She's going to help Mr Price get published. She's reading his book for him. Isn't that nice of her when she's already so busy?'

Davey smiled a nervous smile and backed away, turning the nearest corner and disappearing from sight.

Beatrice tut-tutted and turned back to Eloise. 'I don't know what's got into him. He's always been a bit on the shy side but lately he seems to be even worse. Perhaps it's because Molly upset him by leaving so suddenly. He was quite fond of her, even though she was a bit cruel to him at times.' She let out a little sigh and added as she bustled off, 'It takes all types, though, doesn't it?'

Eloise agreed politely and was halfway up the stairs when she met Mr Price coming down.

'Ah, Dr Hayden, just the person I was hoping to see,' he said with a broad smile. 'I have some suggestions for you for the case you're currently working on.'

She blinked at him once or twice. 'You do?'

'Oh, yes,' he said eagerly. 'I was thinking about it all evening. It's a classic case of a cover-up. He was murdered somewhere else and his body dumped to appear like a drowning. Brilliant, don't you think?'

'Er…yes…'

'I think you need to narrow down your suspects,' he went on. 'You know, the people Mr Jenson was seen associating with in the last hours of his life.'

'That's the job of the local police, Mr Price,' Eloise informed him. 'I'm a forensic specialist called on to give evidence to the coroner. I am not responsible for interviewing witnesses or suspects.'

'Oh…' He looked momentarily deflated but rallied quickly. 'Well, then, you could always do your own investigations, you know, on the sly, or get someone to do them for you.' He puffed out his chest. 'Like me, for instance.'

Eloise had to fight not to roll her eyes in front of him. 'Thank you for your very generous offer but I think it's best if we leave it to the local authorities to deal with,' she said. 'We might end up getting in the way.'

'I can be very discreet.'

She smiled stiffly. 'I'm sure you can, but in this case I think it's best to stay out of it.'

Mr Price began sniffing the air. 'Can you smell that?' he asked.

Eloise suddenly became aware of a faint smell of gas. 'Yes, I can. Has someone left an outlet on or something?' she asked.

'I'll speak to Davey about it,' Mr Price said. 'It happens now and again. There must be a leak somewhere.'

A gas leak?

Eloise began to do the sums in her head.

Ethan Jenson died of a combination of carbon monoxide poisoning and smothering…

Mr Price was already moving past her on the stairs when she swung back around and grasped his arm. 'Mr Price?'

He turned and looked at her. 'Yes, Dr Hayden?'

'Do you know if Ethan Jenson ever came to Trevallyn House? To stay, I mean.'

'I'm not sure but surely Mrs Trevallyn is the one to ask,' he said. 'She knows each and every one of her guests. She makes a point of it. After all, it's her and Davey's home they are renting rooms from. She likes to know exactly who is here and when.'

Eloise quickly excused herself and went in search of Beatrice, who she eventually located sitting in the front room, watching television and eating from a very large box of chocolates.

She closed the lid somewhat guiltily and stuffed them under a cushion when she saw Eloise.

'You won't tell Dr Tremayne, will you?' she asked in a beseeching tone. 'It's my cholesterol. I'm supposed to be cutting down. I allow myself two a day but I just ate five.'

Eloise smiled. 'No, I won't tell. Anyway, I've heard dark chocolate is good for you.'

Beatrice brightened and pulled out the box from beneath the cushions. 'Would you like one? I have peanut brittle or chewy caramel. I'm afraid I've eaten all the soft ones. They're my favourites.'

Eloise took a peanut brittle from the almost empty box. 'I'm a bit of a cupboard chocolate eater, too,' she confessed. Thinking of her mother, she added, 'My thinking is there are worse things to be addicted to, right?'

'Yes, indeed,' Beatrice said. 'My sister was married to a compulsive gambler. He sold everything from under her to feed his addiction—even the toaster and the clock radio went.'

'Oh, dear,' Eloise said. 'That must have been some addiction.'

'It was, but she moved on. She's married to a lovely man now. He's a bit boring but that's neither here nor there.'

'Mrs Trevallyn, I was wondering if you had ever had Ethan Jenson as a guest at Trevallyn House,' Eloise asked once she'd chomped through her chocolate.

Beatrice straightened indignantly on her softly cushioned sofa. 'As if I would allow such a man to sleep in one of my beds!' she said. 'I have very high standards here, as I'm sure you've noticed, Mr Price and yourself being a case in point. I have nothing against surfers, but that young man was a roving tomcat if ever I saw one.'

'So as far as you know he never once came here?'

'No, absolutely not,' Beatrice insisted. 'I don't encourage younger guests anyway. I like the more mature guest. They're far more reliable and never complain about the service.'

Eloise suddenly felt terribly middle-aged and boring.

'Would you like another chocolate?' Beatrice thrust the box under her nose.

'Thanks,' she said, and took two. 'I will.'

The evening was warmer than the night before and the sea breeze only slight. Eloise lifted her face to the air and breathed in deeply. It felt good to be back in her own clothes. She felt safer somehow, as if her armour was back on. She looked down at her dark blue trousers and white linen shirt. They weren't exactly haute couture but they were comfortable and made her feel professional and in control again.

She walked down the steps of Trevallyn House with the intention of avoiding Lachlan before he arrived to collect her, but as if he had sensed her intention, he suddenly appeared at the foot of the stairs.

'Am I too early?' he asked, a little too innocently for her liking.

She gave her head a little toss. 'I was hoping to avoid you.'

He cocked one brow. 'Oh, really? Why was that?'

She gave him a churlish look. 'You know why not.'

He smiled that boyish smile again. 'So I need some work on my pick-up lines. You can coach me through them while we have supper together. I've made a casserole to die for.'

'I wasn't planning on dying tonight.'

'I wasn't planning on killing you.'

Eloise looked up at him. 'Have you talked to anyone about the forensic results?'

He frowned at the gravity of her tone. 'Not apart from my colleagues and Nick Tremayne. Why?'

'There are rumours circulating in the village. I'm concerned that Ethan Jenson's family will hear of the new verdict secondhand.'

He rubbed at his jaw for a moment. 'I was hoping for a bit more time. I'm running with a couple of lines of enquiry but perhaps I'd better talk to the family first. They went to London for a few days but will be back tomorrow, or so I've been told.'

Somehow Eloise fell into step with him along the pathway. 'What are the leads you're working on?' she asked.

'Your findings showed that Jenson was dead prior to being placed in the water. He was seen having a drink with a group of young women at the Anchor Hotel at seven-thirty p.m or thereabouts. The women have all been interviewed and they all said the same thing. Jenson left alone soon after and wasn't seen again until he showed up dead. You said he was in the water by midnight so that leaves approximately four and a half hours in which he was murdered before his body was dumped.'

Eloise glanced up at him. 'So no one knows where he went or who he was with during those hours?'

His forehead was etched in lines of concentration as he continued walking. 'It's as if he disappeared off the face of the earth.'

'Someone must have seen him but they're not telling because they're somehow involved or are worried they might be implicated,' she said.

'That's true enough.'

She stopped walking to look at him again. 'But?'

A sigh whistled out from between his lips. 'But there's something about this that doesn't quite add up,' he said. 'I keep thinking I've missed something along the way. You ever had a case like that?'

'Chief Inspector, they are *all* like that,' she remarked wryly. 'That's what we're paid to do—to make sure things do add up.'

'You can call me Lachlan,' he said with a smile. 'We're off duty, remember?'

'We are?'

'Of course,' he said, reaching for his keys as they approached his house. 'We're just two colleagues sharing a casserole.'

'As long as that's all we'll be sharing.'

'What about a bottle of wine?' he asked as he closed the door. 'Is that allowed?'

'Yes.'

'What about information pertaining to the case?' he added. 'Are we allowed to share that?'

'You know we are,' she said. 'That is, if no one else is listening. Will your daughter be home?'

Lachlan busied himself with opening the wine and finding two glasses. 'She's visiting her mother for a few days.'

Eloise took the glass from him and frowned. 'Did you send her away deliberately?'

'No, it was her idea, actually,' he said. 'Poppy's, that is. She wanted to spend a few days shopping with her mother.'

'I can't help feeling there's something you're not telling me,' Eloise said watching his expression closely.

'I'm getting a little tired of telling you Poppy has got nothing to do with this case,' he said with a little clench of his jaw.

'Where was she the night Ethan Jenson died?'

'She was at home with me.'

She hesitated, then went on. 'Can you prove it?'

'Yes, I can, actually. I had dinner with her about eight and she went upstairs to her room and listened to music until she went to sleep.'

'Did you check on her?'

'I don't usually check on her, but the phone rang at about two in the morning. It was a call from one of the constables working on a case with me in Wadebridge. Poppy woke up then and used the bathroom. We spoke briefly on the landing and she went back to bed.'

'Are you sure she didn't leave the house after that?'

'She was still in bed when I got the call about Ethan Jenson at six a.m.'

Eloise reluctantly backed down. 'All right, I believe you.'

He came over to where she was standing and, using two fingers, slowly lifted up her chin and looked into her eyes. 'You don't like trusting people, do you, Eloise?'

'Every time I have trusted someone they have let me down,' she said in a softened tone.

'So you keep something of yourself back just in case, don't you?' he said. 'You close off the part of yourself that is vulnerable, but in doing so you're not living a full life. It's half a life.'

She stepped out of his hold. 'But it's *my* life.'

'But you're not happy.'

'How do you know I'm not happy?' She looked up at him defensively. 'What right have you got to comment on my private life? How do you know what or who I am?'

'I know because when I kissed you something happened.'

'Nothing happened. You kissed me. I kissed you back. End of story.'

He reached for her, pulling her close to the heat and temptation of his body. 'But it's *our* story, Eloise,' he said, looking down at her mouth with fierce intent. 'It began just over seven days ago and each day is another chapter. Don't you want to see what happens next?'

'I know what happens next,' she said. 'I've read this sort of story before. It's not a novel, it's a short piece of prose. You wave me goodbye in a couple of weeks' time and I never hear from you or see you again.'

'Not according to the version I have,' he said, still looking at her mouth.

'Go on,' she said with a roll of her eyes. 'Tell me what your version is.'

He brought his mouth closer, the movement of his smile against her lips catching on them ever so slightly. 'This is my version,' he said, and covered her mouth with the searing temptation of his.

CHAPTER THIRTEEN

ELOISE wondered much later if she should have at the very least put up token resistance. The thought had crossed her mind but only briefly for as soon as his mouth set fire to hers she was swept away on a rushing tide of need that drove every bit of common sense right out of her head. His tongue danced and darted around her mouth until she was clinging to him, her body screaming out for more.

She kissed him back with escalating excitement, her tongue duelling with his, her stomach leaping and kicking in response as he tugged her even closer to his aroused body. She rubbed against him without inhibition, his low growl of pleasure inciting her to do it again and again.

He backed her into the sitting room towards the sofa, his mouth locked on hers while his hands dealt with her clothes with more haste than care.

Eloise did the same to his, the wild abandon of hearing buttons ping to the floor at their feet thrilling her. Her hands skated over his broad chest as she uncovered it, her fingers exploring the dusting of dark hair before going lower to unfasten his trousers.

His body leapt against her feather-like touch and Eloise wondered if it had been even longer for him than it had for her since the last time he had made love.

She pulled her mouth away from his to anoint his neck and shoulders with teasing kisses, her tongue darting in and out to taste and tantalise him, every movement she made against his skin bringing another guttural sound from his throat.

His pleasure delighted her in a way no one had ever done before. She felt so alive and vibrant, and so very feminine in his arms. Her body pulsed against his, her need matching his as the final barriers of her bra and knickers were tossed to one side.

He looked down at her hungrily, his pupils dilating as he took in her breasts and flat stomach and the gentle curves of her hips. 'I was right,' he said low and deep. 'You look much better without your clothes.'

She gave him a sultry smile as she peeled away his black briefs. 'So do you.'

Lachlan swallowed deeply as she moved down his body in a series of exquisitely tempting kisses, over each of his flat nipples, his sternum, the cave of his belly button and then even further...

He sucked in a breath as she tasted him, her tongue lapping at him in a cat-like manner that lifted every single hair on his scalp. The sensations rose in him with every movement of her mouth on him, the raw intimacy of it taking his breath away.

He pulled away before it was too late and brought her upright to suckle each of her beautiful breasts. He bent his mouth to the right one, drawing delicately on the engorged nipple before increasing the pressure as she clutched at his head and writhed against him.

He moved to the left breast and suckled her, delighting in the whimpering sounds she was making. He moved down her body as she had done to him, lingering over her belly button before moving to the secret heart of her.

She jerked at his first touch, as if it had been a long time since she had felt a man's fingers exploring her neat soft curls. He brought his mouth to her, tasting the sweet honey of her body.

Eloise couldn't believe the impact on her senses at that first intimate stroke of his tongue against her neediness. Her whole body felt as if it was shaking from the inside out, each nerve and pulse sizzling with energy. The first flutters of release came and went, to be replaced by stronger and stronger waves of tension that built to a crescendo until finally she was there, in paradise, her body rocking and rolling with each thunderous wave of pleasure.

She came back to earth with a heavy thud of self-consciousness. Shame coursed through her like a red-hot tide as she met his gaze.

'No,' he said, suddenly straightening and taking her by the upper arms. 'Don't do that.'

'Don't do what?' she asked, trying vainly to tug herself out of his hold.

'Don't go all shy and repressed on me,' he said, frowning at her. 'You enjoyed that. Why should you feel ashamed?'

Tears came to her eyes, which made her both angry and frustrated. 'Because I don't do this sort of thing! I *never* do this…with anyone, or at least not this soon.'

'That makes two of us,' he said sliding his hands down her arms to encircle her wrists. 'I haven't exactly been painting the town red or anything lately. I've been paying lawyer's bills and learning how to be a single dad. I'm ashamed to admit how long it's been. I don't even have a packet of condoms in the house.'

Something loosened in her chest at his gruff confession. 'Oh…'

He gave her a rueful smile. 'Pathetic, don't you think? I'm letting the male side down. I should be out there, having fun every night like everyone else, but until now I haven't even felt the need.'

Eloise ran her tongue across her lips. 'I don't know what to say…'

'I don't suppose you have a condom or two in your purse?' he asked, with another one of those stomach-tilting grins.

'If I have, they'd be well and truly out of date,' she said with a wry twist to her mouth. 'I can't even remember the last time I had sex.'

'Are you on the Pill?'

'Yes, but not for the usual reason,' she confessed. 'I only use it to keep myself regular.'

'So what would you say if we moved to my bedroom and wrote another chapter of our story?'

'I'd say if my foster-parents saw me right now, they would both have myocardial infarcts.'

He laughed as he swept her up in his arms. 'I won't tell if you don't.'

'Put me down, I'm too heavy,' she protested feebly.

His eyes twinkled as he looked down at her. 'Is that a "put me down I don't want to sleep with you" or a "put me down I'm having a fat day"?'

Eloise couldn't help giggling in response. 'It's a "no one's ever swept me off my feet before."'

'Do you like it?'

She gazed into his warm brown eyes and sighed with deep pleasure. 'I love it.'

He carried her through to his room, kicking open the door in such an essentially masculine way she felt her stomach do another somersault.

He laid her on the bed before joining her, his strong thighs draped across hers as he began to kiss her all over again, his mouth wreaking havoc on her already shattered senses.

'You have such a beautiful body,' he said, as he cupped her right breast in his hand, his thumb rolling back and forth over the tight nipple. 'So full and yet so neat.'

'So you *do* think I'm fat.'

He grinned at her mock pout and leaned over to kiss it away. 'I think you're gorgeous, even though you try and hide it all the time.'

She kissed him back and then asked in a musing tone, 'Why am I doing this with you? I feel like I've turned into someone else—someone reckless and shameless and totally wanton.'

He kissed her shoulder and then moved up to her neck, before nibbling on her ear lobe as he said, 'I like the sound of you being reckless and shameless and wanton, especially while you're with me.'

Eloise shivered as his erection brushed against her thigh. Reaching down with her hand, she stroked him boldly, enjoying the satin strength of him against the pads of her fingers.

'Mmm…' he groaned.

'You like that?'

He pressed her back into the mattress and nudged for entry. 'I want you so much I don't think I will last. I'm trying to count backwards and think of sad things to distract myself, but it's not working.'

She smiled and when he looked at her she felt her heart contract. 'You really are a very special lady, Dr Eloise Hayden from Australia. You are so warm and generous under that do-it-by-the-book exterior.'

She wrinkled her brow at him. 'You think I'm uptight and a total control freak, don't you?'

'To be perfectly honest with you, I'm not doing too much thinking at all right at this very moment,' he confessed as he moved against her again.

She lifted her hips slightly and held his gaze. 'I want you to make love to me, Lachlan. *Now*.'

'Is that an order, Dr Hayden?' he asked, with a dancing spark of mischief in his eyes.

'Ye-es,' she said on a swiftly indrawn breath as he surged into her honeyed warmth. 'It is…ohh'

'Am I going too fast?'

'No…no…it's perfect…' she said, on a breath of wonder.

Her body was soaring again, each muscle tightening all over again as she was pitched forwards into oblivion. She clutched at him as she panted her way through it, her skin shivering in reaction as she felt him let finally let go, the sheer force of it pinning her to the bed as he emptied himself.

She stroked his back and shoulders with her hands, exploring him in intimate detail, each knob of his vertebrae, the well-defined muscles that indicated he was a competent swimmer. She went lower to his buttocks, massaging the trim tautness of him before coming back up to his head, her fingers going to his thick curly dark hair, playing with it lingeringly.

'Mmm…' He nuzzled against her neck. 'That's nice.'

'Are you falling asleep on me?' she asked.

He propped himself up on his elbows and looked down at her. 'You know what they say about men who fall asleep after they've made love, don't you?'

She tried to purse her mouth but it turned into a smile instead. 'No, Chief Inspector D'Ancey, what do they say?'

He gave her a playful grin. 'I have absolutely no idea,' he said, and brought his mouth back down to hers.

* * *

Eloise rolled over to her stomach a long time later and idly played with Lachlan's long lean flank lying close to her.

He gave a little shudder. 'That tickles.'

She moved her hand to cup him intimately. 'Does this?'

He stretched like a well-fed jungle cat, even the deep growl that came from his throat sounding primal. 'You're asking for trouble, Dr Hayden. I'm going to pounce on you any minute if you don't stop doing that.'

'I'm hungry.'

He smiled at her. 'For love or for food?'

She let her hand fall away, her expression falling slightly. 'Isn't it a bit soon to be talking of love?' she asked, without looking at him.

He rolled onto his side and turned her face back towards him, his gaze very intense as it held hers. 'I don't know. Is it?'

Eloise felt every second of the pulsing silence as she struggled to think of a suitable answer. She was wary about revealing her feelings but uncomfortable too with allowing him to think she would fall into bed with just anyone to satisfy a physical need.

It was much more than that for her. She hadn't realised how much more it meant to her to be in love with her sexual partner until that moment. It transformed the act into something spiritual and deeply moving.

She moistened her lips. 'I'm not sure…I do know I haven't felt like this before. I'm not sure if it's love or…or something else.' She touched his face with her hand. 'I've never met anyone like you before. I can't believe I'm even lying here with you. It's so out of character for me.'

He kissed the centre of her palm. 'You don't like living in the moment, do you?'

'No…not really.' She gave a little sigh. 'It stems from my

background, I guess. I lived too many days and nights in fear, and eventually those fears were realised. You don't get over that sort of thing in a hurry.'

He brushed her hair back from her face. 'But burying yourself in work isn't going to help you recover, you know. You can't run away from personal demons because they have a habit of coming up behind you and snapping at your heels when you're least expecting it.'

'I know, but I don't want to make the same mistakes my mother made. She hooked up with totally unreliable men. It was almost like another addiction. She just couldn't seem to help herself. I've always sworn I would never take a risk like that.'

'Don't you worry that you will reach the age of forty-five and feel you've missed out on marriage and babies?' he asked.

Her gaze fell away from his. 'I try not to think about it. I would hate a child of mine to suffer some of the things I have seen.' She raised her eyes back to his. 'I just couldn't bear it.'

He brushed her mouth with his lips, softly. 'I know how you feel. Every time I was on a case of child molestation I would be paranoid about Poppy. I drove Margaret mad, telling her never to let her out of her sight. But after a while you realise you can only do so much to protect them. In a perfect world no child would live in danger or poverty, but we don't live in a perfect world.'

'I know, but how wonderful it would be to be able to relax and let go for a while,' she said. 'I feel like I've been living holding my breath for so long. I'm unconsciously waiting for the next phone call telling me of yet another tragic death.'

'Do you ever wonder how different your life would have been if you'd chosen some other career?' he asked.

'Many times, but I can't see myself doing anything else. I try to but I just can't.'

'I'm the same,' he said. 'I love the challenge of a hard-to-solve case. I love that feeling you get when you finally close the file.'

Eloise smiled. 'I've had an offer of help to solve this particular case.'

'Oh, really? From whom? Beatrice Trevallyn?'

'No, but you're close,' she said. 'One of her guests is a wannabe crime writer. He even asked me to read through a couple of his chapters.'

'That would be Mr Price,' he said with a smile. 'He's been coming to Cornwall for years, ten at least. I got roped into reading five chapters of his last novel. I thought it was pretty good, actually. I didn't realise he was already here. He normally comes in July when the weather's more settled.'

'He alerted me to the smell of gas at Trevallyn House,' Eloise said. 'It seems it's a common problem there. I wondered if Ethan Jenson had been there the night he died but Beatrice was adamant he hadn't been. She gave me the whole spiel about men with loose morals never darkening her doorstep and all that.'

Lachlan frowned as something began to niggle at the back of his mind, but before he could figure out what it was the phone rang by the bedside. He had to reach over Eloise to answer it and winked at her playfully as he did so. 'Lachlan D'Ancey.'

A female voice shrieked from the other end of the line, 'How dare you send our daughter back to me pregnant? Poppy said that surfer who died is responsible. What on earth's been going on?'

CHAPTER FOURTEEN

ELOISE froze as the shouted words reverberated around the room. She turned to stare at Lachlan, but he had already risen from the bed and was walking out of the room, carrying the cordless phone with him.

She got up and, stripping the top sheet off the bed, used it to wrap around herself as she went in search of her clothes.

She was so stiff with anger she could barely get her spine to bend low enough to gather her clothes from the sitting-room floor. She dressed haphazardly, not even caring that her white linen shirt was horrendously crumpled.

He came into the sitting room a few minutes later dressed in his trousers, his chest still bare, the phone nowhere in sight. 'I can explain—' he began.

Her eyes flashed livid blue flames of wrath at him. 'Don't bother. I don't want to hear your paltry excuses for withholding such information from me. You do realise what this means, don't you?'

He dragged a hand through his already disordered hair. 'I know it looks bad but—'

'*Bad?*' This time it was her turn to shriek. 'It's worse than bad, Chief Inspector. You are now the number one suspect. Do you realise that?'

He frowned at her. 'That's totally ridiculous. I had nothing to do with Jenson's death.'

She glared at him. 'How on earth do you expect me to believe a word you say? You have lied to me from the beginning. You insisted Poppy barely knew Ethan Jenson and yet apparently she's carrying his baby. Come on, Chief Inspector, give me some credit for having a bit of grey matter between my ears.'

'I don't want Poppy's name destroyed by gossip and innuendo,' he said, still frowning heavily. 'She's too young to cope with this. It would be bad enough if it was just a simple case of a teenage pregnancy, but this is the sort of scenario that could ruin her life.'

Eloise sent him a flinty glare. 'So you conveniently got rid of the culprit.'

Anger flared in his gaze as it warred with hers. 'No, I did not, and I resent you implying that I did.'

She arched her brows. '*You* feel resentful? Hah! What about what I'm feeling? I feel betrayed. Totally betrayed by a man I had grown to admire and trust.'

'I'm sorry, Eloise. I would have told you but I knew you would immediately think I was responsible. Nick Tremayne begged me to tell you but I wanted to wait until I saw how things lay.'

Her eyes widened in outrage. '*Nick Tremayne knows about this?*' she choked.

He gave her bleak look. 'Yes.'

Fury lit her gaze. 'That's two of you I can't trust. I should have known. I had a feeling both of you were holding something back, but I disregarded it at the time, thinking I was being over-sensitive.'

'He was in a difficult position,' Lachlan said. 'He didn't feel he could breach patient confidentiality.'

'He broke it with *you*.'

'No, because Poppy gave him permission to speak to me,' he said. 'She is my daughter and—'

'But this is now a murder investigation!' she railed at him furiously. 'The person responsible is probably laughing at the performing monkeys of the police force.'

His jaw tightened. 'That's an insulting thing to say.'

She cocked one eyebrow accusingly. 'You think I'm being insulting? What about what you just did?'

'I take it you mean the intimacy we shared.'

'Intimacy?' she scoffed. 'Let's tidy up the terminology, shall we, Chief Inspector? Intimacy is where two people connect both physically and spiritually. There is usually an element of trust in the relationship and mutual respect. What we just shared was a cheap roll in the hay, to use a crude expression, although I can think of numerous cruder ones.'

'I understand how upset you must be. But there are instances in life where the rule book doesn't apply.'

She made an impatient sound at the back of her throat. 'Oh for God's sake, I can't believe I'm hearing this from a top-level officer. Don't you have a police manual any more or do you just make it up as you go along?'

His eyes communicated his growing anger. 'There are times when people have to be put before protocol,' he argued. 'Sometimes the bigger picture has to be taken into account. You'd do well to think about that a bit, Eloise. You're so intent on doing everything by the book you're in danger of riding roughshod over people. You came stomping into the village, expecting everyone to stand up and take notice, but you didn't once consider the real victims in all of this.'

Eloise refused to be sent off course by his criticism, even though she felt a sneaking suspicion it might be warranted.

'You deliberately withheld information from me,' she said. 'We're supposed to liaising on this case. How can I trust you after this?'

'This is an unusual situation,' he argued. 'I didn't want to destroy my daughter's life. You surely must understand that?'

'I understand you were after a bit of fun to put me off the scent,' she bit out. 'Nice work, Chief Inspector D'Ancey. While you've been busy seducing me, the person responsible for Ethan Jenson's murder is probably in another country by now. Well done. Another case with "Unsolved" stamped across it.'

'This case is not going to be unsolved,' he said with implacable resolve. 'I have officers working round the clock.'

She snatched up her purse and threw him a filthy look. 'Then I won't waste any more of your time in case there's a remote possibility you take it on yourself to join them,' she said, and stalked out of his cottage.

Lachlan decided against following her. He'd promised to ring Margaret back when she'd calmed down enough for them to talk through Poppy's situation. That had to be his priority for now, but it didn't rest easy with him that Eloise was so angry.

Not after what they had experienced together. He had hoped… Well, that wasn't going to happen now so he may as well get over it.

He let out a jagged sigh, reached for the nearest phone extension and began dialling.

Eloise didn't bother making an appointment to see Nick Tremayne the following morning. Instead, she stormed to the clinic before the consulting hours had begun and demanded the practice manager Hazel inform Dr Tremayne that she was there to see him and would not be taking no for an answer.

He came in a short time later and before Hazel or Sue could even open their mouths to warn him, Eloise had risen from her chair and stalked over to him. 'I have some important questions to ask you, Dr Tremayne,' she said in a don't-mess-with-me tone.

He didn't dissemble but led the way to his office and closed the door once they were both inside.

Eloise went into full swing. 'Chief Inspector D'Ancey informed me somewhat vicariously last night that his daughter is pregnant.'

Something flickered in his dark brown gaze. 'I see.'

'I understand that the father is the late Ethan Jenson,' she went on.

'That has yet to be established,' Nick said.

Eloise's forehead creased in a frown. 'You mean Poppy isn't certain?'

'Her boyfriend Robert Polgrean could just as easily be the father,' he said. 'They've been dating for four years.'

'Have they had a sexual relationship during the whole of that time?'

His eyes hit hers. 'Dr Hayden, their sexual relationship and Poppy's age are issues you will have to take up with Robert Polgrean or Poppy's father. I prescribed a low-dose pill for Poppy a few months back. As to whether she has taken them as prescribed I can't tell you. I do, however, know she only once had intercourse with Ethan Jenson. It's my feeling it's unlikely to be his child, looking at the dates, but she is naturally very upset that it might be.'

'I'm just trying to do my job, Dr Tremayne,' Eloise said. 'But it's not been easy with people hiding important information from me. I realise your dilemma on the issue of patient confidentiality but this is now a murder investigation and Lachlan D'Ancey the officer heading the investigation, is the one—in my opinion—with the biggest motive for killing the victim.'

'I warned him you would immediately jump to that conclusion, but I can assure you Lachlan D'Ancey is not the culprit. He loves his daughter but he would never do anything to jeopardise his career as that would backfire on Poppy. He works damn hard to provide for her.'

'Thank you for the character reference but I will make up my own mind over the authenticity of Lachlan D'Ancey's integrity.'

He shifted his tongue inside his mouth as he surveyed her tightened features. 'You're the first woman he has even looked at since his divorce.'

She put up her chin. 'So he's desperate and dateless. That's not my problem.'

He frowned. 'He's nothing of the sort. Many women have been keen to date him. He's just not been interested. Avoiding a rebound relationship, as far as I can tell. Up till now he's just been concerned about being a good father to Poppy.'

'And what's your excuse, Dr Tremayne?' she asked.

He scowled darkly. 'I told you before I am not going to discuss my private life with you or anyone. I am absolutely furious with Kate that she spoke to you—a person she hardly knows—about something she should have told me years ago.'

'Maybe she was worried you'd react in exactly the way you're reacting now,' she said. 'It's easy for you to judge but you have no idea of what it's like for a woman caught in that situation.'

'Don't tell me what I do and don't know, Dr Hayden,' he bit out. 'I have personal experience of an unplanned pregnancy. Unlike most men, I stuck around and I never once regretted it.'

'Kate obviously cares very deeply for you,' Eloise said. 'The least you could do is take the time to listen to her. It must have been hard, living a lie for all these years.'

He glared her determinedly. 'Thanks for the counselling session, Dr Hayden, but I will handle this in my own way and in my own time.'

Eloise seriously wondered why Kate was even bothering with Nick Tremayne. She had never met a more prickly and arrogant man in her life. 'I am sorry to have taken so much of your precious time,' she said, and hitched the strap of her bag over her shoulder. 'I will be in touch if there are any other questions I need you to answer.'

He didn't respond but as she closed the door behind her Eloise heard him thump his fist on his desk as he swore rather viciously.

'Eloise?' Kate's whispered call sounded from behind her, and she turned to see Kate standing on the stairs leading to her office. 'Can I see you for a minute?'

Eloise smiled and stepped towards her. 'Of course.'

'Not here,' Kate said, and moved down the stairs to join her. 'I need some fresh air. Have you got time for a short walk?'

'I'd like that very much.'

Eloise noticed how Kate seemed to almost tiptoe past Nick Tremayne's consulting room but she visibly relaxed once they were outside in the fresh warm summer morning air.

'I was going to call you to come to my place for dinner this evening. Are you free?' Kate asked.

'I love to come if that's not too much trouble.'

Kate gave her a sideways glance. 'You can bring Lachlan with you if you like. A little bird told me you and he were an item.'

Eloise shifted her gaze. 'Chief Inspector D'Ancey and I are nothing of the sort,' she said crisply.

'Oh…I must have been misinformed.'

Eloise whooshed out a breath and stopped to look at Kate. 'I am so mad at him right now I can barely think straight.'

'Is it about Poppy?'

Eloise hesitated. She wasn't sure how much Kate knew and neither did she want to make Poppy's situation any more difficult than it already was.

'It's all right,' Kate said. 'I know about her pregnancy. I know I'm not really supposed to discuss patient details but in this case I think it's warranted.'

'What a pity Chief Inspector D'Ancey and Dr Tremayne didn't share your view.'

'If it's any consolation to you, Nick was pretty insistent that Lachlan tell you, but he refused. Nick and I discussed it together that day.'

Eloise released a sigh. 'I feel caught in an impossible situation,' she said. 'Lachlan is the first man I've ever felt had something to offer me in terms of a relationship but this has ruined everything. I can't trust him.'

'Don't throw away a once-in-a-lifetime chance at happiness,' Kate said. 'Men like Lachlan don't come along every day. He's a decent man and a very loving father.'

'I'm supposed to be investigating a suspicious death, not on a mission to find a husband,' Eloise said regretfully.

Kate smiled sadly. 'Don't end up like me, Eloise. I am quite a bit older than you and the only man I love is too angry to even speak to me.'

'Hopefully he'll come to terms with it soon,' Eloise offered although from what she'd seen so far she had her doubts. 'It's been a bit of a bombshell and with circumstances as they are with his older children, it's understandable he'd be finding it a bit hard to deal with.'

'Are you going to give Lachlan another chance?' Kate asked after they had walked a little way further.

Eloise looked out to sea, thinking of her apartment so many thousands of kilometres away. 'I have a job to go home to,' she said.

'You can find a job here, Eloise. You're free to do what your heart tells you to do.'

'I'm not sure what my heart is telling me,' Eloise confessed after another few paces. 'I haven't listened to it for a long time.'

Kate gave her arm a gentle squeeze. 'Don't leave it too late, Eloise,' she said, and they walked back to the clinic in silence.

CHAPTER FIFTEEN

'How did your meeting with Ethan Jenson's parents go?' James Derrey asked Lachlan as he came in from another call.

'It was pretty harrowing, as you might expect,' Lachlan answered. 'I took Gaye Trembath with me. She stayed on to sit with Mrs Jenson. We both felt she needed a bit of support.'

'Nasty business,' James said. 'What's next?'

'I want feather samples taken from the Anchor Hotel, where Ethan Jenson was staying, as well as any other place he was known to have spent a night or several hours,' Lachlan said. 'I'll get both Peter Middleton and Dr Hayden to examine them to see if they match the feathers from the lung biopsy Dr Hayden took.'

'Yes, Chief. Anything else?'

'Yes,' he said. 'I want you to find out where Molly Beale is.'

James lifted his brows. 'Isn't she staying at Trevallyn House?'

'No, apparently she left the day Dr Hayden arrived. She didn't leave a forwarding address.'

'You think she's got something to do with this?' James asked.

Lachlan drummed his fingers on the desk for a few seconds. 'I don't know. I know Molly's done a runner before but I want to know if her bank account has been accessed.'

'Have you checked with her mother?'

'I spoke to Maisie Beale earlier,' Lachlan said. 'She threw her daughter out of the house a couple of months ago. Apparently she found Molly in bed with Maisie's new boyfriend.'

James grimaced. 'That must have gone down a treat.'

'It sure did. Maisie insists she never wants to see her daughter again.'

'You don't think…?'

'Molly took her belongings with her when she left Trevallyn House. She didn't have much, mind you, but it always pays to keep an open mind. Our Molly had a bit of reputation with the lads, as I'm sure you know.'

'Did she have a fling with Ethan Jenson, do you think?' James asked.

Lachlan recalled his daughter's distress at hearing Molly Beale had been one of Jenson's conquests so soon after her. 'Yes, I have reason to believe she did.'

James Derrey came back to the station a couple of hours later and took the seat opposite Lachlan.

'Chief, Molly Beale hasn't accessed her bank account or any of her credit cards for over a week,' he said. 'The cards are all up to the max in any case. No one seems to know where she went. She didn't have many friends—I suppose no one trusted her with the silver, not to mention their husbands or boyfriends.'

'I'll go and speak to Beatrice Trevallyn,' Lachlan said. 'It sounds like she was the last person to see her. She might be able to tell me something. You'd better come with me.'

They drove the short distance to Trevallyn House but as they got out of the car the first person to greet them was Arnold Price, who was coming back from a stroll.

'Ah, Chief Inspector, just the person I was hoping to see. How's the investigation going?' Mr Price said with a beaming smile. 'Have you found a suspect yet? I have some suggestions if you haven't. You see, I have this theory—'

'Hello, Mr Price.' Lachlan smiled to take the sting out of his interruption. 'We're here to see Mrs Trevallyn, actually. Do you know if she's about?'

'I think she might be having a nap. I haven't seen her for a couple of hours but, then, I've been out walking thinking through my plot,' he said. 'Shall I get Davey to fetch her? I think he's usually in the garden at this time of day.'

Eloise turned into the gate of Trevallyn House just then to see Lachlan and a junior constable talking to Mr Price, her heart sinking when all three men turned to face her.

'Dr Hayden.' Mr Price was the first to speak. 'How delightful you are all here at the same time. This is absolutely marvellous for my research. Chief Inspector D'Ancey wants to interview Mrs Trevallyn.' He turned to look at Lachlan and added entreatingly, 'I don't suppose I could listen in?'

Lachlan shook his head. 'Sorry, Mr Price. Although this is a routine enquiry, I'm afraid it will have to remain closed to the public.'

'I'll see if I can find Davey,' Mr Price said with another affable smile. 'I don't like to go to Mrs Trevallyn's room on my own. She's bit old-fashioned that way.'

'I understand,' Lachlan said, and once the elderly gentleman had gone round the side of the house he turned to Eloise. 'Dr Hayden, this is PC James Derrey. James, this is Dr Eloise Hayden from Australia.'

Eloise shook the younger man's hand. 'It's nice to meet you, James.' And with a little glittering glance cast in Lachlan's direction she turned back to James and added, 'And you can drop the Dr and the bit about coming from Australia. I prefer to be called Eloise.'

'Oh…right, then,' James said, looking a little flustered as he took in the silent exchange between his chief and their international guest.

'What did you want to see Beatrice about?' Eloise asked Lachlan after a short, tense pause.

'I want to interview Molly Beale, the cleaning maid who worked here previously. So far we haven't been able to locate her.'

'You think she's somehow involved in this?' Eloise asked, not realising she was practically repeating verbatim with what James had asked not half an hour earlier.

'It's too early to say,' Lachlan answered. 'I would like to know her movements on the night in question and take it from there.'

'You'd better come in and wait in Beatrice's sitting room,' she said, unlocking the front door, but as soon as she stepped inside she reeled backwards from the strong smell of gas.

Lachlan had smelt it too and dragged her backwards and called out for James to call the fire service.

'What if Beatrice is inside?' Eloise asked, frowning in concern.

'Stay here and I'll check,' he said.

'No, I'm a trained doctor,' she said. 'She might be unconscious.'

'We'll all be unconscious if we don't take care. Now, stay here.'

Eloise stood her ground, whipping her hand out of his iron hold. 'No, I will not stay here. If she and Davey are unconscious, they'll need to be moved, and you can't do that on your own. We can put handkerchiefs over our mouths and see where they are.'

Mr Price came up the front steps, puffing heavily. 'I can't

find Davey and the back door is locked.' He sniffed the air and frowned. 'Is that gas?'

'Yes, it is. Please, stay well back until the fire crew gets here,' Lachlan ordered. 'Eloise, take this handkerchief and double it over your mouth. If at any stage you feel faint or nauseous, you are to leave the building immediately—is that understood?'

She nodded, folded the cloth over her mouth and followed him into the guest-house.

Lachlan checked each room, opening every window he came to while keeping a close watch on Eloise a step behind him.

They found Beatrice first. She was lying on the floor of one of the smaller rooms upstairs. Lachlan rushed to the window while Eloise dropped to her knees and checked for a pulse. 'She's alive,' she said.

Lachlan found Davey the other side of the single bed, still with tools in hand in front of the faulty outlet.

'Davey's over here,' he said, and bent down to examine him. 'He was obviously trying to fix the leak when he lost consciousness.'

Eloise came over and examined Davey quickly, relieved to find a pulse, although it was a little thready. 'We need to get them both to hospital or the clinic at least in order to give them oxygen.'

James appeared at the door with a couple of firemen, who had already turned off the gas at the mains.

The patients were soon transported to the clinic and after Nick Tremayne had assessed them, they were given oxygen until the ambulance arrived to transport them to St Piran Hospital.

Kate came over to where Eloise was awaiting a final decision by the fire crew about the safety of staying at Trevallyn House.

'I'm afraid they're going to close it down temporarily,'

Kate said. 'It seems the gas pipes have needed replacing for years but poor Bea never had the money. You can stay with me. Jem will love it.'

'That's very kind of you,' Eloise said. 'What about Mr Price?'

'Lachlan's taken care of that,' she said. 'He's got a spare room.'

'Mr Price will be beside himself,' Eloise said with a wry look in Lachlan's direction, where he was still speaking to Nick.

Lachlan turned as if he'd felt the weight of her stare and came over to speak to her. 'Dr Hayden, I've organised for some pillows from the Anchor Hotel and a couple of other places, as well as Trevallyn House, to be tested for a match with the feathers found in Ethan Jenson's lungs.'

'Thank you, Chief Inspector,' she said in a crisp, professional tone. 'I was just about to suggest we take some samples from the guest-house.'

One of his brows lifted in surprise, or was it admiration? Eloise couldn't really tell. 'Were you, now?' he asked.

'Yes,' she said. 'I smelt gas the other day and it occurred to me there might be a connection, but so far I haven't been able to establish one. Not unless Molly Beale secretly took Ethan Jenson up to her room. Beatrice Trevallyn was adamant he had never been there but that's not to say…'

He glanced at Kate, who was hovering near by. 'Let's leave our discussion till you examine the samples,' he suggested. 'Give me a call when you're done at the lab.'

'Right.'

He strode away with a brief nod and smile at Kate on his way past.

Kate whistled through her teeth as she came back to Eloise. 'I'd say he was done like a dinner.'

Eloise frowned. 'What on earth do you mean?'

'The way he looked at you just then,' Kate said with a knowing smile. 'I'd say you'd better organise for the rest of your things back home to be sent over straight away. That man is in love.'

'That man is a jerk,' Eloise said irritably. But she couldn't help glancing in his direction when she hoisted her bag over her shoulder and made her way outside to her car.

Dr Middleton looked up from the lab's microscope some hours later. 'They found a match,' he said. 'Have a look and see what you think.'

Eloise came over and examined the samples carefully for several minutes and eventually came to the same conclusion. 'You're right, Dr Middleton. The sample from Trevallyn House exactly matches the feather particles I took from the lung biopsy. We'll ask them to do a cross-check to make sure, but I think it's starting to add up.'

After a series of cross-checks were done and the results documented, Eloise called Lachlan on his mobile and arranged to meet him in his office. Her tone was matter-of-fact but inside she was a jangling mess of nerves, hurt and heartache.

When she arrived at his office, she stood outside his door for several moments, trying to get her chest to loosen enough to breathe. *You can do this*, she reminded herself sternly.

She clenched her hand into a fist and raised it to the door's surface, but it suddenly opened and her hand landed on Lachlan's chest with a little thump.

'Maybe I should think about getting a doorbell,' he said with a twisted smile.

Eloise's hand dropped back to her side but she could still feel the warmth of his chest against her knuckles and her chest gave another flutter.

'I have a match,' she announced briskly, once they were both seated. 'Trevallyn House—in fact, the very pillow from the bed Molly Beale used.'

'I thought you might.'

She looked at him closely. 'Have you found out what happened yet?'

'Davey woke up a couple of hours ago,' he said. 'He told us everything. It seems Molly asked him to distract Beatrice so she could bring Ethan Jenson up to her room that night. It hadn't been the first time either. The arrangement was that Ethan would wait upstairs in her room while Molly finished the dinner things downstairs. Then she would come up and they would presumably have sex and then with Davey's help Ethan would be escorted off the premises, all without Beatrice finding out.'

'Did he tell you what happened that particular night?' she asked.

'Yes he did. Poor chap. He's distraught, of course, but Molly threatened him so much he did what she suggested. He was terrified his mother's home and livelihood would be taken from her. You remember I told you about a salmonella outbreak a while ago?'

She nodded.

'Well, Davey was frightened he might have to be institution-alised or something if his mother could no longer keep the guest house going. You have to remember he thinks like a young child.'

'Yes, I realise that. It's very sad.'

'Apparently the arrangement went as planned. Ethan Jenson left the Anchor Hotel around seven-thirty and Davey let him in and locked the door to Molly's room with Jenson inside. That was to stop other guests inadvertently opening the wrong door apparently. Jenson waited upstairs but Molly got held up with some extra work. When she got to her room

Ethan was lying face down on the bed and there was a strong smell of gas. She told Davey she quickly turned off the gas at the wall and opened the window before she tried to find a pulse, but when she couldn't find one she hatched a plan to get them both off the hook.'

'Clever of her,' Eloise remarked cynically.

He gave a shrug. 'Molly isn't exactly a rocket scientist and certainly Davey wouldn't have been much help. Why they didn't call an ambulance at that point I guess we'll never know. Ethan might have been able to be resuscitated. He may have only just lost consciousness.'

Eloise inwardly winced at the thought of Ethan's parents being informed of the possibility their son might not have died if help had come sooner. 'What happened next?' she asked.

'Molly told Davey if he didn't get rid of Jenson's body he would be charged with murder because he was the one who brought him into the house and locked him in the room. So that's what Davey did. He took Ethan down under cover of darkness and dumped him in the ocean.'

Eloise frowned as she tried to take it all in. 'And no one saw him? Ethan Jenson was five eleven and of average weight. It would have been hard to disguise him as something else.'

'Davey is often seen about at odd hours carrying old bits of rubbish about the place. He does some gardening jobs for a couple of retired folk down near the harbour. If anyone saw him, they'd think nothing of it. He's often got a sack of some kind on his back.'

'But what about the smell of gas at Trevallyn House?' Eloise asked. 'Surely Beatrice would have been able to smell it that evening if not some of the other guests.'

'Beatrice Trevallyn has no sense of smell. She had a mini-stroke a couple of years ago and as a result lost her ability to smell. As for the other guests staying there…well, there weren't any at that time. Mr Price hadn't yet arrived and you didn't come until early June. The place is often empty as it's a bit run-down. Davey did his best but really he should have contacted the gas people much earlier. One can only assume he was worried about the expense of refitting the pipes.'

'Have you located Molly Beale to get a statement?'

'Yes, she was found about an hour ago in Glasgow. She gave a frank and full confession. She was lying low, hoping things would settle down. That was why she left the day you arrived. When she heard a police doctor was coming from Australia she knew she had to get away, and fast, and not leave a trail. She used what cash she had on her but, of course, it eventually ran out. We got her on her first cash-card transaction.'

'She was taking a very big risk, trusting Davey to keep quiet,' Eloise commented.

'Davey's been infatuated with her for years,' he said. 'He would do anything for her. It's my guess she played on it for all she was worth.'

A silence swirled around them for several long seconds.

'Will charges be laid against both of them?' she asked.

'I would hazard a guess that Davey won't be charged on the basis of his disability. Molly will be charged with perverting the course of justice. She's already pleaded guilty. The coroner's going to reopen the inquiry at short notice on account of you being here from abroad. He'll need you to present your findings. I think the inquiry will be in about ten days' time.'

'So we were both wrong,' Eloise said after another small pause. 'You thought it was drowning and I thought it was a straight case of murder.'

'Yes,' he said, looking at her mouth. 'We were both wrong.'

Eloise swallowed as another protracted silence thickened the air.

'Eloise, there's something I want to ask you.'

'No, please,' she said, forcing herself to meet his gaze. 'Don't.'

He frowned at her. 'You don't want to even consider the possibility that we could have a relationship, do you?'

'I live in Sydney, you live in Penhally Bay.'

'You could move.'

She tightened her mouth. 'Why don't *you* move?'

His frown deepened. 'Because I have a daughter and an ex-wife who expects to see her reasonably regularly, that's why. I also have a grandchild on the way. I can't move...or at least not right now.'

'And yet you expect me to drop everything and take up with you—for how long? Six months, a year?'

'I hadn't got as far as putting a time frame on it,' he said. 'We've known each less than two weeks.'

Eloise wondered if he was having a dig at her for falling into bed with him so readily. She hoped not. She *desperately* hoped not. 'Lachlan...' She moistened her lips and tried to get her voice to co-operate by sounding normal instead of choked up with emotion. 'I think I made a mistake... I mean, I *know* I made a mistake by sleeping with you. I gave you completely the wrong impression. It was a mistake, one of my biggest, actually.'

He frowned at her. 'The biggest mistake you'll ever make is walking out that door without giving me a chance to put things right between us.'

'You can't put things right that were wrong from the word go,' she said, steeling herself for his counter-attack, which she knew was going to undo her completely unless she kept her emotions under tight control. 'I was a fool to be tempted. I'm ashamed of my weakness. It's totally unprofessional and it could have jeopardised the whole investigation.'

'But it didn't, Eloise,' he said. 'We solved this case working together, looking at it from different angles. We could make a great team. Please, take the time to think about it. You have to stay around for the coroner's inquiry in any case.'

Eloise felt as if her heart was being clamped by a huge vice. She wanted to say yes to everything, but how could she know it would work out? He had just ended a miserable marriage. It would be unfair of her to expect him to jump straight into a new one if, in fact, he had the intention of asking her, which she very much doubted.

She would be risking everything she had worked so hard for—her career, her professional reputation, and the one thing she had protected so guardedly for so long. Her heart.

'Please, Eloise,' he said. 'At least think about it for a week or two. Don't you owe me that?'

Eloise felt as if every part of her was being stitched into a tight knot of pain deep inside her. Her chest felt weighted, as if a stone had settled there, pushing her heart to one side so it couldn't work properly. 'I don't owe you anything, Lachlan,' she said in the same controlled tone, even though she was as close to tears as she had ever been. 'We had a brief fling and as far as I'm concerned that's the end of it.'

'I'm not going to make a fool of myself, begging you to change your mind,' he said. 'Neither am I going to tell you I love you because I'm not sure if what I feel is the real thing, but it sure as hell feels like it.'

'You're still getting over your ex-wife,' she said, even as her heart gave a sudden leap of hope before settling down again. 'You're vulnerable right now. Any man would be.

Especially with Poppy in the situation she is in. You're not able to think clearly.'

He let out a sigh and sent a hand through his hair. 'Maybe you're right,' he said, giving her a wry smile. 'I'm not exactly doing this the textbook way, am I?'

She gave him a small smile in return. 'Maybe you should book in for some lessons or read a book or something.'

'*Dating for Dummies*. Now, that just might be the way to go,' he said with one of his disarming grins.

She reached up and kissed him on the cheek before her common sense muscled in to stop her. 'You're a good man, Chief Inspector D'Ancey. There are a lot of women out there who would give an arm and a leg to be with you.'

His mouth twisted ruefully. 'But not you?'

She let out a heartfelt sigh. 'What you need is a hearth-and-home type, someone to have your dinner ready when you come home from another tough day at the station. Not someone who is slaving over blood splatter samples and lying awake most nights, having nightmares about the victims' last moments of life.'

He reached out and touched her softly on the cheek with the back of his knuckles. 'You take care of yourself, Dr Eloise Hayden from Australia,' he said softly.

She swallowed back the emotion rising in her throat and gave him a stiff little smile. 'I will,' she said. Moving out of his embrace, she left the room and closed the door quietly but firmly behind her.

CHAPTER SIXTEEN

'How do you feel now the coroner's inquiry is over?' Kate Althorp asked close to three weeks later.

Eloise slumped as she sank into the nearest sofa chair. She had been staying with Kate and Jem since Trevallyn House had been closed for the repairs to the gas system to be completed. Beatrice and Davey had both recovered and had gone to recuperate with Beatrice's sister and her husband in Devon. Beatrice had decided to sell the guest-house and move into something smaller with Davey, which seemed a good solution all round.

'I'm fine. I feel a bit sorry for Molly Beale, however,' Eloise answered. 'When she goes to court she'll probably get three years for perverting the course of justice, but she might get out earlier if she behaves herself. She might even benefit from being inside for a short time. No charges were laid against Davey. A psychiatrist declared him unfit to stand trial.'

'What about Ethan Jenson's parents? How did they seem to handle it all?' Kate asked.

Eloise puffed out a sigh and laid her head back on the sofa cushions. 'I've talked to them a few times,' she said. 'As you can imagine, it's agonising for them. They can't help thinking that if only Molly or Davey had stopped and called for help when they first discovered him, Ethan might be alive today.'

'Everyone is wise in hindsight,' Kate said. 'But I guess they panicked at the time.'

'Yes, that's true, although he was definitely dead when he hit the water. At least he didn't suffer. Drowning is not a pleasant way to die, although I guess it's better than some other ways.'

Kate fiddled with her watch for a moment. 'I thought you might like to know Lachlan is back from London. He brought Poppy with him.'

Eloise gave her an offhand glance. 'I don't see what that has to do with me.'

'She had a miscarriage while she was in London with her mother,' Kate said. 'That's why Lachlan wasn't at the inquiry. He sent a signed affidavit instead.'

Eloise had assumed he had taken leave to avoid running into her at the inquiry where she had been called to present her evidence. She hadn't thought for a moment there might be some other reason he hadn't shown up. She'd been so angry that he hadn't even bothered to phone her, but now she realised he would have been totally preoccupied with his daughter, offering his support and trying to help her get over an extremely traumatic time.

'Is Poppy all right?' she asked.

'Physically, yes, but a bit fragile emotionally, or so Lachlan said. No one in the village knows about it, of course, apart from Nick and Robert, who has been a real sweetheart to her. I'm only telling you because she wants to see you before you leave tomorrow.'

Eloise looked at Kate in surprise. 'She wants to see me? But what on earth for?'

'I don't know, but she called a few minutes ago, before you came home. I think Robert is driving her over right now.'

Eloise chewed at her lip and frowned.

'Are you going to see Lachlan before you leave tomorrow?' Kate asked into the silence.

Eloise shifted her gaze. 'I don't really see the point.'

Kate gave her a lengthy look. 'Are you sure you're doing the right thing by leaving with things so up in the air between you?'

Eloise got to her feet and began to pace the room. 'I can't stay here without some sort of commitment from him, Kate. I don't know what he's told you, but we had a brief fling. It was little more than a one-night stand,' she said, trying to convince herself that was all it had been.

'He didn't speak of it in quite those terms,' Kate said.

Eloise swung around to look at her. 'What did he say?'

'Not much. He didn't betray any confidences or anything. He just said how much he had enjoyed being with you and that he was going to miss you. Also that you made him realise what he had been missing out on in his marriage to Margaret.'

Eloise frowned. 'Nothing else?'

Kate shook her head. 'Why, were you expecting something else?'

Eloise whooshed out a breath and crossed her arms over her chest. 'I don't know... I guess a marriage proposal might have made me think twice about leaving.'

Kate's eyes went wide. 'I thought you were a career-woman to the backbone? No marriage, no kids—or have I got it wrong somewhere?'

'Yes, well, I was totally career focused until I met Chief Inspector Lachlan D'Ancey,' Eloise confessed. 'Ever since then I keep having these crazy thoughts about a white dress and a long veil and...and...'

'And?'

Eloise scowled. 'Never mind. It's stupid anyway. My flight's booked and I'm almost packed.'

'You can always cancel the flight and unpack your bag.'

'I could but I won't.' The doorbell rang and Eloise added as she went to answer it, 'Kate, you've been so kind over the last couple of weeks. I really appreciate it, especially as you've got your own issues to deal with right now.'

'They've waited several years,' Kate said resignedly. 'I guess they can wait a little longer.'

Poppy was standing on the doorstep looking pale and thin, nothing like the surly street-wise teenager Eloise had met four weeks ago.

'Hello, Dr Hayden,' she said with a wavering smile. 'I hope this isn't an inconvenient time for you?'

'No, it's fine. I wasn't doing anything special tonight, just packing.'

'You're leaving tomorrow, right?' Poppy asked, her brown eyes containing a flicker of worry.

'That's the plan.'

Poppy shifted from foot to foot. 'Um…are you free to come for a little walk? Robert's waiting in the car for me. It won't take long.'

Eloise looked to where Robert was sitting behind the wheel of his run-down car. He lifted his hand in a small wave and turned back to the car magazine he was reading. 'Sure. Why not?' she said. 'You lead the way.'

Poppy led the way to the bay past the lifeboat station and down onto the sand. 'I always like to take my shoes off on the sand, don't you?' she asked. 'I like the feel of it squishing between my toes.'

'Yes,' Eloise said, wondering what this was all about. Poppy seemed as if she wanted to get something off her chest and although Eloise hadn't been expecting any last-minute friendly overtures, she thought that as the young girl had been through a rather traumatic time, she at least deserved a hearing.

Poppy took off her sandals and looked at them for a moment. 'I have a huge apology to make,' she said, dragging her gaze up to meet Eloise's. 'I was so rude to you the first time I met you. And that day at the café when I totally ignored you. I know you probably think I'm a horrible person, but really I'm not. I was just very confused and upset.'

Eloise smiled. 'You're a teenager, Poppy. Sixteen is a tough age. I remember it all too well. You're not quite an adult but you want to be one.'

'I had a taste of being an adult and I can tell you I'm not quite ready for it,' Poppy said, biting down on her lip. 'I'm not sure if you know, but I had a miscarriage. I made Dad promise not to tell anyone. Only Mrs Althorp and Dr Tremayne know…and Robert, of course…'

Eloise saw the glisten of moisture in the young girl's eyes and placed a gentle hand on her arm. 'Do you want to talk about it? It sometimes helps to talk to someone other than a family member.'

Poppy sniffed and wiped her nose on the back of the sleeve of her light cotton shirt. 'It's OK. Dad's been great,' she said. 'Mum's been better since…since…I…lost it. She was so angry at me. I wanted her to hold me and tell me things were going to be OK, but all she could do was shout at me for wasting my life and throwing my career options away. She wanted me to have an abortion. She kept pressuring me. She even made me an appointment at a clinic. I was so confused. I just wanted to turn back the clock and make it all go away… And then I started to bleed…'

'You poor darling,' Eloise said softly.

Poppy gave her a wobbly smile. 'I wish you would stay a little longer and give my father a chance. He pretends he's OK but I know he's not. It's my fault, isn't it? If I'd been nicer to you from the start, maybe you wouldn't be flying back to Australia tomorrow.'

'Poppy, it's not your fault at all,' Eloise insisted. 'Things just…just didn't work out.'

'Why? Don't you like him or something?' Poppy asked, looking at her intently.

Eloise gave her a crooked smile touched with regret. 'I like him, Poppy,' she said. 'I like him a lot.'

'Enough to marry him?'

'That's a completely hypothetical question.'

'Because he hasn't asked you?'

Eloise let out a breath in a slow but uneven stream. 'No, no, he hasn't.'

'Would it make a difference if he did?' Poppy asked.

'Listen, Poppy, your father's just come out of his marriage to your mother. The last thing he needs right now is a new wife.'

Poppy poked at a bit of seaweed with her big toe. 'It'd be all right with me, you know…if he did ask you, I mean. I know I said I didn't want another mother but I like you. You make my dad smile. I love my mum and all that, but I can see now why they couldn't make a go of things. Mum's too driven. She can't stop and look at the big picture. She's really happy with Roger. They're both as career mad as each other. Dad loves his work, he would never have gone as far as he has without some sort of dedication and ambition, but he still always finds time for me. When he heard I was losing the baby, he dropped everything to come to me, even though the inquiry had just started.'

'You're a very lucky girl to have such a wonderful

father,' Eloise said, feeling wretchedly guilty for misjudging him so badly.

Poppy smiled. 'I think so, too. I just want him to be happy. He's only thirty-nine, that's not really old.'

'No, it's not.'

Another little silence passed, broken only by the whisper of the water lapping gently at the shore.

'I feel so guilty about the miscarriage,' Poppy said after another few paces. 'Guilty but relieved.' She stopped and looked at Eloise again. 'Do you think that's terribly wrong of me?'

'No, of course it's not wrong to feel that way,' Eloise answered. 'It must have been such a difficult time for you. You need to put it behind you now and get on with your life.'

'Yes…that's what Robert said.'

They walked a little further in silence until Poppy looked down at the sand near her toes. 'Hey, look,' she said. 'Someone's written a message on the sand with shells.'

Eloise looked at the first couple of letters and wrinkled her brow. 'It doesn't make sense. What does *aila* mean?' She peered a little closer and asked, 'Is that next letter to it *r* or *n*?'

Poppy looked down. 'It's definitely *r*,' she said, and then, visibly brightening, added, 'Hey, this is fun. Robert and I used to do this. We'd leave coded messages for each other on the beach. Here's another one. I think that's *t*—or is it *f*?'

Eloise crouched down. 'I'm not sure. I think someone's walked across that section.' She straightened and walked a bit further to where the shells began again and started reading the rest of the letters out loud. '*Susmorf…*' She looked up at Poppy again with a puzzled expression. 'What does *susmorf* mean?'

'Um…I think there's meant to be a gap between the *s* and the *m*,' Poppy said, suddenly biting her lip.

Eloise frowned again. 'It still doesn't make sense.'

'There's more over here,' Poppy said. 'Look.'

Eloise looked, her eyes narrowing slightly. 'Hang on a minute…' She leant down a little closer. '*nedyaH…esiolE.*' She straightened and met Poppy's gaze. 'That's my name spelt backwards.'

'Oh, yes.' Poppy looked back at her with big innocent brown eyes. 'So it is.'

'And there's an *r* and D for Doctor.' Eloise looked at Poppy again. 'What's going on?'

Poppy gave her a sheepish look. 'Maybe we should have started at the other end,' she said. 'I think I might have got Dad's directions wrong.'

Eloise's eyes narrowed even further. '*Your father wrote this?*'

Poppy nodded and started to walk quickly back the way they had come. 'I think I can hear Robert calling me,' she called over her shoulder. 'I'll meet you back at the car.'

Eloise would have gone after her but the need to read the rest of the message was too great. She walked along and mentally rotated the words so they made sense. '*Question mark…me…marry…you…will…*' She stopped when she came to a large pair of bare feet and slowly looked upwards into a pair of whisky-brown eyes.

'Someone went for a jog over the last bit,' Lachlan said with a rueful smile. 'I'm not sure if it makes sense any more.'

Eloise blinked at him, her heart starting to race and her legs feeling as if they were as soggy and waterlogged as the sand at the water's edge a few feet away.

He stepped closer and took both of her hands in each of his. 'Will you marry me, Dr Eloise Hayden from Australia?' And with a boyish grin added, 'Or is it Ausfnalia?'

She laughed and threw herself into his arms, her heart feeling as if it was going to burst with joy. 'I don't care what or where it is—I'm staying here with you.'

He swept her off her feet and swung her around, the shells of his proposal crunching under his feet. 'Do you mean it? Do you really mean it?' he asked.

'Yes.' She was crying and laughing all at the same time. 'Of course I mean it. I know it's crazy and too soon for you and too soon for me and my career is probably going to take a nosedive, but I love you. I think I've been fighting it from the start, but I can't stop how I feel any more.'

'I love you too, darling,' he said. 'I should have told you earlier but I only realised it today. The thought of you getting on that plane and never coming back was too much to bear. I suddenly realised I was in love with you, *really* in love with you, which meant I had to find a way to ask you to marry me in a hurry.'

She hugged him around the neck and showered his face and mouth with kisses. 'That was a very creative way to propose.'

'Actually, it was Poppy who gave me the idea,' he said. 'And all was going well until that wretched jogger went past. He had feet like planks.'

'Just as well the tide didn't come in,' she said, smiling at him delightedly.

'I had already covered that contingency, although I must confess I had a bit of trouble locating enough shells. There must have been a few kids down here today, collecting them.'

'At least I saw it and answered it,' she said with a heartfelt sigh. 'That's all that matters.'

His brown eyes twinkled. 'Yes, but do you know what they say about messages written in the sand, Dr Hayden?'

She grinned from ear to ear. 'I don't know. What *do* they say, Chief Inspector?' she asked.

He smiled at her tenderly. 'They say they last for ever,' he said, and brought his mouth down to hers.

* * * *

BRIDES OF PENHALLY BAY

Medical™ is proud to welcome you to Penhally Bay Surgery where you can meet the team led by caring and commanding Dr Nick Tremayne. For twelve months we will bring you an emotional, tempting romance – devoted doctors, single fathers, a sheikh surgeon, royalty, blushing brides and miracle babies that will warm your heart…

Let us whisk you away to this Cornish coastal town – to a place where hearts are made whole.

Read on for a sneak preview from
Virgin Midwife, Playboy Doctor
by Margaret McDonagh
– the eighth book in the
BRIDES OF PENHALLY BAY series.

VIRGIN MIDWIFE, PLAYBOY DOCTOR
by Margaret McDonagh

Oliver watched for a moment as his final patient of the day hobbled along beside her boyfriend, then he went back inside and, after exchanging a few words with the receptionists, he returned to his desk in the consulting room that had been made available for his use while he was there. The previous occupant, Lucy Carter, married to Ben, an A and E consultant at St Piran, and daughter of the surgery's senior partner, Nick Tremayne, was on maternity leave.

Sighing, he set about the task of updating his patient notes and dealing with the ever-present pile of paperwork, but his attention wandered in a predictable direction. To Chloe. Whose room was immediately above his own. His gaze lifted, as if somehow by staring at the ceiling he could see her, will her presence. She was all he seemed to think about these days. And she scarcely appeared to know he was alive. It was a novel and not very pleasant experience.

He had only been in Penhally Bay a short time, but he had been drawn to Chloe from the moment they had met on his first day in his new job. And he meant what he had said earlier. Chloe was an excellent midwife…the best he had worked with. He admired her skill, her kindness, the way she always went that extra mile for the mums-to-be who meant so much to her. Like today, accepting Avril's need for another opinion and putting herself out to drive the obviously panicked woman to hospital. Perhaps he had been working too long in an impersonal big city practice. His time back in Cornwall had opened his eyes again to the true meaning and enjoyment of proper community medicine.

London had been a blast. At first. He'd had the brains to breeze through medical school, had enjoyed a successful career and an active social life since qualifying and, thanks to his family's success, he'd had the money to live life to the fullest. A cynical smile tugged his mouth. There had been good times, but his lifestyle had had its downsides, too. He was tired of those who were impressed by the family name, the bank balance, the exaggerated reputation. Tired of being used. He wanted to be seen for himself, the person he was, and not for the added trappings or as a prop to give someone else a good time. He had become mistrustful, dubious of people's— women's—motives.

He had grasped the opportunity to come back to Cornwall, his home county. His family was here, although thankfully far enough away from Penhally to allow him privacy. He loved them. They loved him. They had just never understood him. Never understood his need to make his own way and not be swallowed up in Fawkner Yachts like his grandfather, his parents, his brother and his sister. It had always been medicine that had drawn him, excited him, not the family business.

Being back in Cornwall had added benefits. He could indulge his passion for surfing and jet-skiing on an almost daily basis. And already he felt reconnected, enjoying his work in a way he had not done in the cut-and-thrust impersonal world London had become for him. Having made a conscious decision to change his life, the plan had been to settle in Penhally Bay and lie low while he established himself. He had no experience of long-term relationships, had never lived with a woman, but it was one of the things he most wanted...to find a nice girl, to settle down, to have a family. Eventually. What he had not anticipated had been meeting anyone who interested him so soon. And Chloe MacKinnon more than interested him.

She was unlike anyone he had ever known. He had never felt like this about a woman before and he was wary, unsure of venturing into the unknown. In the future, he wanted something different, some*one* different, and from all he had seen and heard so far, Chloe fitted the bill in every way. Just thinking about her made him smile and sent the blood pumping faster through his veins, a curl of heat flaming in his gut.

Melanie Milburne

QUESTIONS & ANSWERS

Would you like to live in the fictional Cornish town of Penhally Bay?

Most of my fans know how passionate I am about the beach so I can think of nothing better than living in a small coastal village like Penhally Bay, as long as each pub sells Tasmania Sparkling wine, however!

Did you enjoy writing as part of the Brides of Penhally Bay series?

I thoroughly enjoyed being a part of this series; it had its challenges at times as the plot was a complex one, dealing with both tragedy and romance. I found it fascinating to learn about the science of forensic pathology. The only downside is I have now become one of those annoying "experts" who point out all the procedural mistakes in crime shows!

What was it like working with other authors to create the backdrop to these books?

Writing is a bit like marathon running – it is a lonely existence at times, so I really loved working with the "Penhally gang." We each did our own thing with the characters and plot we had been given but we touched base many times to check details, which made the writing process less solitary.

How did you first start writing romance novels?

I had just finished my Master's thesis and wanted to

do something completely different. I still can't quite believe I am a multi-published author. I was supposed to be an academic. I had my PhD all mapped out when I sold my first book but I am having too much fun now to change tack.

What do you love most about your hero and heroine in *Single Dad Seeks a Wife*?

I love that they are both experts in their professional life but struggle with their personal lives. It shows how none of really get it all to hang together perfectly, but then we are human after all.

Can we have a sneak preview of your next book…?

My next Medical™ is *The Surgeon Boss's Bride*. It is about a top Sydney neurosurgeon, Ben Blackwood, who finds out his new registrar, Georgie Willoughby, is the daughter of the professor who failed him in his Fellowship several years ago. The sparks fly from their very first meeting. It was a joy to write, as Georgie is so enthusiastic about everything she does and Ben is of course knocked sideways by her in more ways than one! I hope you enjoy their journey to find true happiness, as I certainly loved writing it.

4 Books
and a surprise gift!

We would like to take this opportunity to thank you for reading this Mills & Boon® book by offering you the chance to take FOUR more specially selected titles from the Medical™ series absolutely FREE! We're also making this offer to introduce you to the benefits of the Mills & Boon® Reader Service™–

- ★ FREE home delivery
- ★ FREE gifts and competitions
- ★ FREE monthly Newsletter
- ★ Exclusive Reader Service offers
- ★ Books available before they're in the shops

Accepting these FREE books and gift places you under no obligation to buy, you may cancel at any time, even after receiving your free shipment. Simply complete your details below and return the entire page to the address below. You don't even need a stamp!

YES! Please send me 4 free Medical books and a surprise gift. I understand that unless you hear from me, I will receive 6 superb new titles every month for just £2.99 each, postage and packing free. I am under no obligation to purchase any books and may cancel my subscription at any time. The free books and gift will be mine to keep in any case.

M8ZEF

Ms/Mrs/Miss/Mr ....Initials..
BLOCK CAPITALS PLEASE
Surname ....
Address...

....
....Postcode ....

Send this whole page to:
UK: FREEPOST CN81, Croydon, CR9 3WZ